'I have some

'The only thing [...] gritted, 'is that y[...] you're going to talk to your sister and get her on the first plane back to England. Frankly, I've had all I can stand of both of you. If you're still here by tomorrow night, I'll report you both to the authorities!'

Dear Reader

As the dark winter nights unfold, what better to turn to than a heart-warming Mills & Boon! As usual, we bring you a selection of books which take you all over the world, with heroines you like and heroes you would love to be with! So take a flight of fancy away from everyday life to the wonderful world of Mills & Boon—you'll be glad you did.

The Editor

Stephanie Howard was born and brought up in Dundee in Scotland, and educated at the London School of Economics. For ten years she worked as a journalist in London on a variety of women's magazines, among them Woman's Own, and was latterly editor of the now defunct Honey. She has spent many years living and working abroad—in Italy, Malaysia, the Philippines and in the Middle East. Currently, she lives in Kent.

Recent titles by the same author:

THE PHARAOH'S KISS
COUNTERFEIT LOVE
CONSPIRACY OF LOVE

A SCANDALOUS AFFAIR

BY
STEPHANIE HOWARD

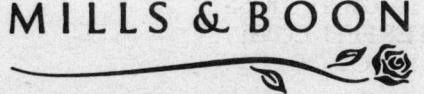

MILLS & BOON LIMITED
ETON HOUSE, 18-24 PARADISE ROAD
RICHMOND, SURREY TW9 1SR

All the characters in this book have no existence outside the imagination of the Author, and have no relation whatsoever to anyone bearing the same name or names. They are not even distantly inspired by any individual known or unknown to the Author, and all the incidents are pure invention.

All Rights Reserved. The text of this publication or any part thereof may not be reproduced or transmitted in any form or by any means, electronic or mechanical, including photocopying, recording, storage in an information retrieval system, or otherwise, without the written permission of the publisher.

This book is sold subject to the condition that it shall not, by way of trade or otherwise, be lent, resold, hired out or otherwise circulated without the prior consent of the publisher in any form of binding or cover other than that in which it is published and without a similar condition including this condition being imposed on the subsequent purchaser.

First published in Great Britain 1993 by Mills & Boon Limited

© Stephanie Howard 1993

*Australian copyright 1993
Philippine copyright 1993
This edition 1993*

ISBN 0 263 78300 6

*Set in Times Roman 11 on 12 pt.
01-9312-47657 C*

Made and printed in Great Britain

CHAPTER ONE

'Wow! Did you ever see anything like that?'

It was the man standing behind her in the DJ who had spoken.

Luisa smiled as she answered him. 'No, never in my life!' Then she turned back to gaze out over the still waters of the Caribbean to the huge sleek white yacht that lay at anchor there, lighting up the night sky with a thousand twinkling lights. From its decks, across the balmy, sweet-scented air, drifted the sounds of music and laughter. You could almost hear the champagne corks popping!

Luisa smiled to herself as she kept her gaze fixed on it—though the gleam in her eyes was one of satisfaction, not admiration. The information she had received had been correct, she was thinking. Tonight Roth Elman was throwing a party.

Behind the man in the DJ she stepped into the motor launch—one of a whole fleet of them that had been laid on specially to ferry guests from Nassau harbour to the party—and seated herself among her glittering fellow passengers. And no one would have guessed that the slender blonde-haired girl, looking relaxed and confident in a slinky green silk evening gown, in her heart was almost dying of trepidation.

For Luisa could scarcely believe what she was doing. Never in her life before had she gatecrashed a party! And this was no ordinary party she was headed for. This glittering event was the sort of affair someone like her would never be invited to in a million years!

Not that the party was really what interested her. What interested her was the party's host, Roth Elman. He didn't know it yet, but she had a bit of unpleasant business to do with him.

Luisa clenched her fists as the launch approached the yacht. Somehow, she must slip on board the yacht undetected. She must give the impression she had every right to be there. She must act as though she were a legitimate guest. And she could do it, she told herself, if only her nerve held.

And her nerve *must* hold. She snatched a calming breath. There was too much at stake to allow her anxiety to overwhelm her. She focused on that. This might be her only chance to confront Roth Elman and save her sister's family.

They were alongside the yacht now. Luisa rose to her feet and made her way behind a woman in a red velvet dress towards the flight of steps that led up on to the main deck. Mentally, she crossed her fingers and prayed.

It seemed someone was listening. Miraculously, a minute later, she was being helped on board by a smiling young crew member.

He touched his white cap. 'Welcome aboard, miss!'

Luisa smiled at him, disbelievingly. 'Thank you,' she answered. Inside, she was cheering. She'd done it! She'd made it!

But through her triumph, her stomach clenched. Now came the hard part!

More than an hour had passed since Luisa's arrival on board the yacht, but she still hadn't come face to face with Roth Elman.

That could wait, she had decided, as soon as she'd realised that the situation was a little less straightforward than she'd been expecting. Before confronting Elman, a bit of investigation was called for—which was why, on tiptoe, she was creeping round the fore deck, peering through portholes, poking her head round doors, her heart beating inside her, amazed at her own daring.

But her investigation, so far, had yielded nothing, and she was on the point of giving up as, with a sigh of resignation, she pushed open the door of yet another empty cabin, stuck her head round and whispered, 'Rita? Are you there?'

As silence greeted her, she was about to withdraw again. But then a sudden small sound from the far side of the cabin caused her for a moment to stop in her tracks.

'Rita?' she whispered again, her eyes straining against the darkness. She took another step forward. She had definitely heard something.

Nothing moved. Nothing stirred. The only sounds were the sounds coming from the aft deck, the sounds of a party in full swing.

Luisa stopped and stood still, peering into the darkness. Perhaps she had imagined it, she was thinking. She sighed, lost in thought, distracted, for a moment, wondering what she ought to do next.

And then, from the open doorway, startling her, a voice spoke. 'I don't think you'll find what you're looking for in here.'

Luisa knew before she spun round who the voice belonged to. Her heart caught in her throat. Her cheeks flushed then grew pale. I'm in big trouble now! she thought as she turned to face him.

'Ah, Mr Elman! You surprised me!' Her tone sounded plausibly innocent, she reflected, mildly horrified at her powers of deception. 'I had no idea you were there.'

'No, I can see that.'

He was standing just inside the doorway, his back to the light, his face in shadow. All Luisa could make out against the moonlight was a tall male silhouette, broad-shouldered and faintly menacing. But in her mind's eye she could see the piercing dark eyes and feel them drive through her like red-hot pokers.

She shifted uncomfortably, feeling the need to explain herself, cursing herself for allowing him to catch her. She took a deep breath. 'I thought I heard a noise,' she said.

'A noise? What kind of a noise?'

'I don't know. Just a noise.'

'And, hearing this noise, you felt the need to investigate?'

Luisa dropped her gaze involuntarily. That was not how it had happened. She'd already been in the throes of investigating when she'd heard that sudden, unidentified noise! She observed obliquely, avoiding an outright lie, yet knowing she could scarcely tell him the truth, 'I'm beginning to think I may have imagined it. There doesn't seem to be anything here.'

'Let's see, shall we?'

As he spoke, he flicked the light switch and suddenly the cabin was flooded with light.

Luisa blinked as she found herself looking into his face. Suddenly there he was, standing right before her—Roth Elman, arch-villain, business tycoon and media superstar. She was aware of a nervous tightening deep inside her. All at once, uncontrollably, her heart was racing.

For, though she was familiar with the features of his handsome suntanned face with its razor-sharp cheekbones, strong curved nose and thrusting jawline, she'd been unprepared for the impact of seeing him up close. There was a power about this dark-haired, thirty-five-year-old man that made the very air around them seem to shimmer.

Luisa looked at him and thought, This man eats life—and heaven help anyone who's on the menu!

His eyes were watching her, eyes as black and hard as jet stones. 'There,' he said. 'Now we can see what we're doing.'

Luisa cleared her throat. 'Yes, that's much better,' she agreed. 'I can't think why I didn't do it myself.'

'I can't think why, either.' He raised one dark eyebrow and curved his shapely mouth in a smile without humour. 'Unless, of course, you were hoping not to be seen.'

'Hoping not to be seen?' As her heart skipped guiltily, Luisa detached her gaze swiftly from the curving, shapely mouth that really was the most sensuous mouth she had ever seen. 'Why on earth would I be hoping that?'

A pair of equally sensuous coal-black eyes flicked over her. 'I suggest that that's for you to tell me.'

Earlier, as Luisa had watched him mingle with the party guests, she'd been aware of the physical dynamism of the man. With every move he made, however fleeting, however subtle, he projected an aura of radiant vitality. And, even now, she could feel it as he stood there in the doorway, his lean, powerful frame propped against the door-jamb in an attitude at once casual and supremely arrogant.

But what had escaped her before was the sheer sensuality of him that seemed to soften and yet subtly enhance his sparkling power. She could feel these combined forces reaching out to her, drawing her against her will, as seductive as sin.

Potent stuff, she found herself thinking. Little wonder my sister fell for him!

That thought sobered her instantly. She said, narrowing her eyes at him, 'I already told you... I thought I heard a noise.'

'Ah, yes, the noise. I'd forgotten about the noise...'

He paused and fixed her with his midnight-black eyes, allowing them to sweep unhurriedly over her, taking in everything, every soft-skinned feature of her intelligent, wide-eyed, heart-shaped face with its frame of glossy, shoulder-length blonde hair. Then he continued his impudent scrutiny, his gaze gliding over her naked shoulders and all the way down to her green silk shoes, making her skin burn as though it had been touched by hot cinders. Luisa was unable to suppress the shiver that ran through her.

'Well, whatever the noise was, I can't see anything to worry about.' As he spoke, to her relief he detached his gaze from her person and cast a quick glance round the cabin. 'There doesn't seem to be anything here.'

'No, there doesn't.' Luisa quickly pulled herself together, hating the way her skin was still burning. Impudent, arrogant beast to look at me like that, she thought. For it had been the look of a tiger lazily eyeing up a gazelle, mentally earmarking it for some future hungry moment. She made herself a promise. I'll never be Roth Elman's dinner!

Then, following his gaze, she added, 'As I said, I must have imagined that noise I thought I heard.'

'Indeed you must. How very odd.' With a lift of one eyebrow he swept his dark gaze back to her. 'Are you in the habit of imagining noises?'

Luisa smiled to herself. This was typical Roth Elman. That cool, confrontational tone of voice as he'd posed the apparently innocuous question was one she'd heard him use countless times on TV during his favourite pastime—bullying journalists. She'd seen many a fellow-journalist crumble in the face of it. She squared her shoulders. She would not crumble.

'No,' she answered levelly. 'I do not make a habit of hearing noises.'

The tall lean figure in the formal black suit shifted slightly in the cabin doorway, causing a shaft of light to glance across his shoulder, casting an almost bluish sheen over the glossy jet-dark hair.

He smiled at her arrogantly. 'That's most reassuring. At least from your point of view, I imagine it must be. Hearing imaginary noises would pose a problem for anyone...' He paused. 'But for a journalist it could prove a serious professional handicap.'

Luisa felt her heart judder. 'How did you know I was a journalist?'

'How did I know?' His eyes pierced through her. 'Why, was it supposed to be a secret?'

'Not particularly.' Luisa looked back at him, struggling to hang on to her composure. It wasn't really the fact that he knew she was a journalist that had caused her horrified reaction. It was the fact that he knew anything at all about her! Her presence on the yacht was supposed to be a secret. He wasn't even supposed to know she was here!

'Not particularly.' He repeated her denial in a tone of total open scepticism. 'Then perhaps you would have been wiser to keep it a secret. You see, I never invite journalists to my parties.'

'Oh.'

'Oh, indeed. You see, I dislike journalists. In fact, you could say I dislike them a lot.'

Never had a truer word been spoken! His dislike of journalists was legendary!

Luisa glanced down at the floor and cursed herself silently. Earlier, never suspecting that it would ever reach his ears, when one of the guests had asked her what she did for a living, she had answered truthfully that she was a freelance journalist. There had seemed no point in lying. Her job, after all, was in no way connected with her reasons for being here.

I'm just no good at all this cloak-and-dagger stuff, she thought now, miserably, half wishing she'd never allowed herself to get talked into it in the first place.

As she glanced up again, Roth was watching her, smiling coldly. 'So, you'll appreciate that in the circumstances I find myself wondering how on earth you happen to be here. My parties are strictly by invitation only. And I know—we both know—that I didn't invite you.'

Luisa hesitated, suddenly immobilised by her own sense of discomfort. I should never have got into this, she thought again. But then she looked into the unwavering hard dark eyes and forced herself to remember why she *had* got into it.

In order to try to save her sister Rita's family from being torn apart by this very man! Surely that more than justified telling him a couple of harmless lies?

She took a deep breath. 'I came with friends of yours,' she told him.

'Friends of mine?'

'Yes.' In fact, in a way, that was true. The group she'd attached herself to in the motor launch and in whose company she'd slipped on board the yacht, she had gathered from their conversation, were legitimate acquaintances. But she was stretching the truth as she went on to elaborate, 'We didn't think you'd mind if I tagged along.'

'Are you saying my friends invited you?' The inquisitorial eyebrow lifted. 'Who are these friends? Kindly name them.'

Luisa scrabbled to remember the names she'd heard on board the motor launch—and came up with two. 'César and Victoria.'

'César and Victoria.' The dark eyes narrowed thoughtfully. 'I wasn't aware that either of them had friends in journalism.'

'Perhaps you don't know your friends as well as you think you do.'

'Perhaps I don't.' He smiled. 'You could be right.' A look of lazy amusement touched his eyes. His gaze flicked over her, dark and sensual, causing an odd sensation to trickle down her spine. He has eyes that can touch you like hands, Luisa thought.

Then the smile became cold again, his eyes as sharp as hatchet blades. 'Perhaps I don't know my friends as well as I think I do...' He straightened slightly, his gaze driving into her. 'And perhaps you don't know them at all. Shall we go and ask them?'

Luisa felt a coldness touch her. This game wasn't funny. She hated the deception she was being forced to perpetrate. With every fibre of her body she wanted to confess. And, indeed, originally, that had been her intention—to confront him openly with her reason for coming here. But she'd been forced rather hurriedly to revise that plan. For the moment at least, her best strategy, she sensed, would be to keep her purpose hidden.

She looked into his face now, fighting her feelings, reminding herself that this was no game she was playing, and challenged him, 'We can ask them if you wish.'

To her utter astonishment, the bluff appeared to work. He had seemed on the point of escorting her back to the party, but instead, slipping his hands into his trouser pockets, he observed, 'I understand your name's Luisa. Luisa what?'

'Luisa Baker.'

'Luisa Baker.' As he paused and narrowed his eyes at her, Luisa sensed she knew what he was doing. He was running her name through the computer that was his brain. For she knew Roth Elman had a computer for a brain. A sophisticated, ruthless, cold computer. She had seen it in action many times on the small screen.

'And you're from England. I can tell that from your accent. So, what are you doing in the Bahamas, Luisa Baker... apart from accompanying Victoria and César to parties?'

'Holidaying. What else?' If only it were true! And it would have been true, she would have been holidaying, if this business about Rita hadn't cropped up. Not here in the Bahamas—this place was beyond her pocket!—but it had been her plan, after completing her business in New York, to spend a couple of weeks in New Orleans.

'So, you're a guest of César's and Victoria's?' His tone was impenetrable. It was impossible to tell whether he believed her or not. 'That appears to be what you're telling me... that you're holidaying with them.'

Luisa looked at him without answering for a moment. She flicked back a stray strand of hair across her shoulder. Then, neither confirming nor denying his suggestion, she answered brightly, 'They're a lovely couple, aren't they? So generous and friendly.'

'Indeed they are.' The dark eyes were watching her, as he continued to stand there in the cabin doorway. 'And their home in Nassau is quite exquisite. I almost envy you spending time there.'

Luisa's stomach had tied itself into tight, guilty knots. She could scarcely believe she was indulging in this charade. She had to remind herself once more why she was doing it—and of the fact that the last person she should feel guilty about lying to was this villain who stood before her. The odious Roth Elman.

Yet she avoided a direct lie. 'You know it, do you—their home in Nassau?'

'Very well. I've been there many times. But not since the new extension was built. I understand that's quite a triumph?'

'Absolutely. That's what it is. A triumph.'

Roth nodded and smiled, then straightened slowly. Good, thought Luisa, he's going to release me. He's swallowed my story and now we're going to go back to the party.

But then he took a step towards her. 'How about a drink?' he suggested.

'A drink?' Luisa blinked and stepped aside awkwardly, as he proceeded to sweep past her to the other side of the cabin. And for the first time she noticed the contents of the cabin—a comfortable-looking bunk bed in one corner, a desk, a wardrobe and, beneath the curtained window, a small bar at which Roth Elman had now taken up position.

He glanced at her over his shoulder. 'What would you like?'

Luisa shook her head. 'I don't really want anything.' Or rather, what I would like, she amended silently, is to end this confrontation, not turn it into some sort of social event!

'I'm having a whisky.' As he spoke, he proceeded to pour one. 'Tell me what you'd like. I can't drink alone.'

That remark was accompanied by a warm, slow smile and a glance that was little short of a caress. They were the smile and the glance of a seducer, Luisa told herself, fending them off with a steely glare. She would not be seduced by him—though it struck her again that it was easy to understand why her sister Rita had somewhat rashly kicked over the traces for this man.

'Well?' he demanded again. 'What will you have?'

There was no point in resisting. She might as well just go along with him. And why not? Why not play the part of innocent guest being offered a private drink with her host? After all, that was what she wanted him to believe she was.

She forced herself to relax. 'I'll have a tonic, thanks.'

'Ice and lemon?' As she nodded, he turned to look at her. 'Are you sure you wouldn't like something a little stronger?'

'No, thanks.' Though it struck her that a stiff shot of vodka might be precisely what she needed. After all, she'd been sticking to tonic water all evening—in order to try to keep a clear head—and look where her abstinence had got her!

He seemed to read her mind. 'Absolutely sure?'

'Absolutely.' Now, more than ever, she needed to have her wits about her. She had no idea why he was suddenly being so charming, but she did know she didn't trust him an inch.

Roth stepped towards her and handed her her drink, his fingers brushing against hers for the most fleeting of instants. Had he done that deliberately? Luisa wondered, snatching her hand away, surprised at the jolt of electricity that shot through her from her scalp right down to the tips of her toes.

He was saying, 'This is an excellent idea. A bit of peace and quiet for five minutes.' As he spoke, he took a mouthful of his drink and lowered his tall frame on to the edge of the desk. 'Quite frankly, I'm not a great lover of parties.'

'Aren't you? Now that surprises me.' Luisa did not believe him for a moment. 'I would have thought you were a keen party-goer.'

'And why would you have thought that?' He turned on her that smile that felt like warm velvet brushing against her skin.

Luisa pushed the feeling from her. 'I was watching you earlier,' she told him. 'You looked to me as though you were in your element.'

'Did I, now?'

'Yes, you did.'

The way he'd moved among his guests, effortlessly drawing the eyes of all who were gathered there, he'd appeared like a star moving among lesser dull planets. He'd seemed to dominate the crowd by the simple fact of his presence.

He smiled again. 'Perhaps I'm always in my element.'

'Perhaps you are.' She could not resist smiling back at him. Such bare-faced arrogance was oddly disarming.

But she was disarmed only momentarily. Instantly, she reminded herself that Roth Elman was a contemptible and thoroughly dangerous man.

She swirled her tonic water round in the glass. 'Well, I'm surprised to hear you don't like parties.'

'Oh, I enjoy the occasional party. I wouldn't deny that.' Luisa could feel his eyes on her as he answered. 'But I'm not what you'd call a regular party-goer.' He paused. 'Not like your friends, Victoria and César.'

Luisa glanced up, feeling her stomach shrink inside her as he added, 'Now they're what I'd call dedicated party-goers.'

She said nothing.

'But I'm sure that's something you already know... since you're such good friends of theirs and a guest in their house.'

A chill touched Luisa's skin. His expression had never altered. He had made the remark as though it was just conversation. Yet it hung in the air now, ominous and threatening. She had the feeling that a trap was closing round her.

Her fingers tightened around her glass. 'Yes, I suppose they are,' she said.

'Oh, very definitely they are. They'd be the first to admit it.' The dark eyes scanned her stiff, nervous figure. 'Why don't you sit down? Take the weight off your feet?'

There was an armchair at her side and Luisa would gratefully have sunk into it, except that she suspected that once seated in its depths she would simply feel even more trapped than ever.

She straightened her spine and swirled her tonic water. 'If you don't mind, I prefer to stand,' she answered.

'Suit yourself.' He continued to watch her. Then, still in that casual tone, he demanded, 'How long have you been friends with César and Victoria?'

'Not long.'

'How did you meet them?'

'The way one meets people. By accident.'

'By accident?'

'By accident. I don't remember the details.' She swirled the tonic water faster and faster. 'What is this?' she shot at him. 'Some kind of interrogation?'

'Interrogation? Of course not. I'm just curious, that's all.' He took another infuriatingly calm mouthful of his whisky and settled himself more comfortably on the edge of the desk. 'You see, there's something I just can't quite figure out...how you come to be a guest in their home in Nassau when I happen to know they haven't been there for weeks... They flew in specially for the party from New York this afternoon.'

Luisa felt her heart grow still. I have two alternatives, she told herself. I can make a dash for the door, throw myself overboard, head for the shore and probably drown in the process... Or I can stay here, make another final attempt to talk my way out of this and probably end up being eaten alive for my efforts.

As choices went neither held much appeal, but at least, if she stayed, there remained a crumb of hope that she might still achieve the purpose she had come here for!

With a sigh she sank down on the arm of the armchair, then took a deep breath before raising her eyes to his. 'Look, Mr Elman, I'm afraid I've been less than honest.' She pulled a face. 'I owe you an apology. I'm not a friend of César's and Victoria's. I'd never set eyes on them till I met them in the launch coming over...'

As she paused, Roth Elman drained his whisky. He looked straight at her. 'Now tell me something I don't know.'

At least he was listening. He wasn't ripping her to pieces. Luisa glanced down into her tonic water and swirled it slowly. 'Mr Elman, I apologise. I gatecrashed your party. I——'

'I already know that, too. I told you to tell me something I don't know.' The casual tone had gone now. There was a warning in his voice. 'Tell me, for example, *why* you gatecrashed my party.'

But she couldn't do that. Not yet, anyway. Luisa swallowed and blurted out the only excuse she could think of.

'It was a spur-of-the-moment thing. An impulse, really. I heard some people at my hotel talking about the party. It sounded like it was going to be the party of the year...'

She broke off, regretting that clumsy attempt at flattery. He wouldn't fall for flattery. That wasn't how to get round him.

But what was? She swirled her drink faster and faster. 'I don't know what possessed me. It was just a crazy impulse. Suddenly I wanted to come to the party more than anything.'

'I see.'

'I know I shouldn't have. I know it was wrong. But I didn't mean any harm. Really. I promise you.'

'So, you're telling me that to enjoy the party was the only reason you came?'

Luisa nodded. That indeed was what she was telling him, though, alas, of course it wasn't true. It's only a temporary measure, she told her squirming conscience. In the end he'll know the truth.

Swallowing hard, she told him, 'Yes, that was why I came.'

'Well, I suppose I can't really blame you.' Roth smiled a tolerant smile and laid his empty whisky glass down on the desk. 'After all, as you said yourself, it's the party of the year.'

As he spoke, he began to rise to his feet. Was he about to release her? Luisa felt her tension slacken.

'There's just one other thing...' He stood over her for a moment. 'What were you doing prowling about the fore deck?'

'I wasn't prowling.' Her heart was racing as her mind flew in all directions, searching for some plausible-sounding excuse. She was so close to liberation. She mustn't blow it now!

'I really just felt like a breath of fresh air. I wanted to get away for five minutes from all the noise and the people. I didn't mean to trespass. I'm sorry if I did.'

The black eyes were watching her, boring into her. Nervously, Luisa swirled her drink.

'And that noise you thought you heard, that brought you into the cabin...?'

'I must have imagined it. I don't know what it was...'

'I don't know either.' He slipped his hands into his trouser pockets again. 'But I suppose in your shoes I would have done the same. I mean, if I'd heard a noise, I would probably have wanted to investigate...'

'It was a natural impulse. I just opened the door without thinking.'

'I'm sure you did.'

'And I can see that it looked suspicious.' She went on swirling without thinking. 'But really, Mr Elman, I——'

Suddenly, she broke off and jerked away from him, her heart jumping like a startled frog as he reached out towards her. What the devil was he about to do?

Then an instant later, as confusion gripped her, she felt the cold splash of tonic in her lap as the contents of her glass emptied over her dress.

'I saw that coming.' Roth was shaking his head, as she leapt to her feet as though something had scorched her. 'The way you were fiddling with that glass it was just a matter of time before you emptied the whole lot over yourself.'

He paused and looked down into her flushed, confused face. 'I was about to relieve you of the glass in an effort to avoid an accident, but alas instead I made the accident happen.'

Only because of the foolish way she had reacted. Luisa glanced down at the dark stain on her green silk dress. 'What a mess,' she murmured dismally. The dress agency was going to love it when she returned the dress to them tomorrow in this sorry state!

'It shouldn't leave a mark if you dab it lightly with some water.' Roth broke through her thoughts and nodded towards the *en-suite* bathroom. 'You'll find some towels and things in there.'

It sounded worth a try. Luisa nodded. 'OK.' She really would prefer not to spend the rest of the evening in a dress with a stain all down the front!

Through in the tiny bathroom she dabbed the wet mark carefully. It would dry quickly once she was outside in the balmy night air, and with any luck it might not show at all.

'I think it'll be OK. It...'

As she stepped back into the cabin, Luisa frowned and looked around her. Where was Roth? The cabin was empty.

He's probably waiting for me outside, she decided, pushing back her hair and heading for the door. Or else he's gone back to the party, leaving me to find my own way. Either way, it looked as though her ordeal was over. He had evidently swallowed her story.

Her hand was on the door-handle, a sense of relief rushing through her. For the rest of the evening she must be ultra-careful not to arouse his suspicions again. He wouldn't let her off so lightly a second time.

But, even as she prepared with a confident smile to step through the cabin doorway and head back to the party, she could feel her optimism shrivel inside.

She was going nowhere. The cabin door was locked.

CHAPTER TWO

LUISA was awakened ten hours later by a light tap on the cabin door.

She leapt from the bunk bed, sprang across the room and demanded furiously as she flung the door open, 'What the devil do you think you're playing at?'

But standing before her was not Roth Elman, as she had expected, but a young uniformed steward who instantly took a step back.

'I'm sorry to disturb you, Miss Baker,' he told her, 'But Mr Elman wonders if you'd care to join him on the sun deck for breakfast?'

Luisa pulled the towelling bath-robe round her shoulders and offered the young man a smile of apology. 'I'm sorry,' she told him. 'I didn't mean to be rude. Please forgive me. I thought you were someone else.' Then she took a deep breath. 'Please tell Mr Elman I'll be with him as soon as I've showered and dressed.'

The steward nodded politely. 'He said to give you this.' He held out a plastic-covered hanger. 'In case you need it, it's a change of clothes.'

Luisa smiled to herself as she withdrew back into the cabin. Nice touch, she was thinking. She did indeed need a change of clothes. Sitting down to grapefruit and a bowl of corn flakes in her green silk ballgown might have looked a little odd!

She slipped off the towelling bath-robe she had found in the bathroom and which she had decided to don two hours into her incarceration, when it had finally become clear that, even if they could hear her, no one was about to respond to her cries for help and that it would require more strength than she possessed to batter down the door. Even the window offered no possibility of escape. It, like the cabin door, was firmly locked.

So, weak with anger and frustration, she had eventually flopped down on the narrow bunk bed, cursing Roth Elman and her own stupidity, and pretty soon had drifted off to sleep.

And now, she realised, as she stepped from the shower, her shoulder-length blonde hair wrapped in a towel, she was absolutely ravenous with hunger. Little wonder, she acknowledged as she peeled the plastic from the hanger to reveal a pair of shorts and a simple cotton top, plus a pair of rubber flip-flops in a bag; it was almost twenty-four hours since she'd had a square meal. Yesterday evening she'd been too nervous to eat and last night at the party she'd never had a chance!

The shorts were a little on the big side, but they did the job. Luisa unwrapped her hair and pulled a comb through it—a comb, a lipstick and a twenty-dollar bill were all she'd brought with her in her dainty green silk bag. She had not been expecting to stay overnight.

Her lips firmed as she glanced at her reflection in the mirror. Roth Elman had some explaining to do. How dared he have the gall to make a prisoner of her? She would demand that he end this farce immediately and return her to dry land as soon as she'd had breakfast!

A couple of minutes later, she was storming up the sun deck to confront the figure, all dressed in white, who was seated alone at the breakfast table there.

Eyes flashing, she stood in front of him. 'I have a bone to pick with you!'

He turned lazily to face her, sensuous dark eyes skimming over her. 'Good morning,' he said. 'I trust you slept well?' He waved to the chair beside him. 'Do take a seat.'

Even first thing in the morning he looked heart-wrenchingly handsome, Luisa found herself thinking with a dart of annoyance. She scowled at him. 'First things first. I would like you to explain...'

But in mid-sentence she stopped, her eyes widening in horror, as she stared past him disbelievingly at the horizon.

She gulped. 'Where are we? Where's Nassau disappeared to?'

Then, before Roth could answer, she was rushing to the guard rail, then dashing across to the other side of the yacht. But, wherever she looked, there was no sign of land anywhere. They appeared to be miles from anywhere, in the middle of the sea!

Shocked and belatedly aware of the throb of the engines, Luisa felt all the colour drain from her face. She turned back to face Roth again. 'You're kidnapping me!' she accused.

He seemed to find that amusing. He smiled. 'I don't think so.'

'You don't think so!' It was not the most reassuring answer. Luisa glared into his handsome, hateful face, her fists bunched angrily at her sides. 'Then, kindly tell me, what *are* you doing?'

'Having breakfast.' He smiled again. 'Why don't you join me?'

Luisa flashed him a grim look. 'Where are we?' she demanded.

'A few miles south-east of Providence Island, at a guess.' With uncaring impudence he lifted his coffee-cup and drank. 'If you want a more precise location you'd better speak to my captain.'

'I suppose you think that's funny?' Luisa was almost speechless. She had known the yacht was due to sail today—that was why she'd had to gatecrash last night's party!—but she'd never dreamt for one moment that it would sail with her on board.

And now, here she was, marooned in the middle of nowhere, with a man she wouldn't trust as far as she could throw him. Suddenly she felt distinctly uneasy.

'What game do you think you're playing?' she demanded, trying not to sound scared. 'Are you in the habit of locking up your guests for the night, then setting sail without even a word to them?'

One jet-black eyebrow lifted slowly as he looked at her. 'I think you've got one essential detail wrong there. You, Miss Luisa Baker, were never my guest.'

'A slip of the tongue.' Luisa narrowed her eyes impatiently. 'So, is that why you locked me up? Is that why you're taking me——' she glanced around her '—to the middle of nowhere? Just because I gatecrashed your stupid party?'

'Not entirely.' Roth continued to watch her with just a hint of that amused smile of before. 'I had a couple of other reasons as well.'

'For example?'

'For example...' He let his eyes drift over her, causing her skin to tingle strangely. 'For example, I'm really rather keen to discuss the reason *why* you gatecrashed my party.'

'I see. And are you in the habit, Mr Elman, of making prisoners of the people with whom you wish to discuss things?'

He smiled, amused. 'Only those who seem reluctant to tell me what I want to know.'

'I already told you what you want to know. I already told you why I gatecrashed.'

'Yes, you did.' He paused to take another mouthful of coffee. 'Unfortunately, however, I don't believe you. You didn't gatecrash my party on some silly impulse, just because the idea appealed to you. You had a reason.' His eyes impaled her. 'And I intend to discover what it was.'

As he delivered this pronouncement he had turned back to his breakfast and was helping himself to waffles and syrup. Luisa regarded the dark profile that now was turned against her—the strong nose, straight brow and jutting chin—and once again she was struck by the power he exuded. In the end, even if she resisted, he would extract the truth from her, so perhaps it would make more sense just to co-operate now.

And, besides, it no longer made any sense to go on resisting. It was pointless trying to keep her reason for being here hidden. And the sooner he knew the truth, the sooner he would release her!

'OK.' Unclenching her fists, Luisa crossed to the table and seated herself obligingly on the chair opposite him. 'I'll tell you what you want to know.'

'I see the clothes fit not too badly.' He took a mouthful of waffle and cast a look of appraisal across the table. 'The shorts are a bit on the big side, as I knew they would be. Remind me after breakfast to lend you a belt.'

'That won't be necessary.' Luisa felt a dart of irritation at the swift and impressively accurate summing-up. Not many men of her acquaintance had such an eye for female dressing. But then Roth Elman was probably an expert in all areas female!

She reached for the jug of orange juice and poured herself a glassful. 'I'd hate to put you to any more trouble. Besides, as soon as I've had breakfast, I'll be leaving.'

'Is that so?' He smiled amusedly. 'You'll be leaving, Miss Baker, when I say you can.'

Luisa felt a dart of worry, but regarded him boldly. 'Once I've told you what you want to know, you'll have no reason to keep me.'

'Won't I?'

'In fact, I suspect you'll be glad to see the back of me.'

'Will I, indeed? That sounds most promising.' He washed down the waffle with another mouthful of coffee. 'I confess I can't wait to hear what you have to tell me.'

He was a sarcastic bastard. Luisa regarded him with disapproval. Many times on TV she had watched and writhed in sympathy as he'd systematically demolished some poor innocent interviewer whose debating skills were not quite up to his own. With that acid tongue of his and that rapier-sharp intelligence, he could grind all but the most intrepid into the ground. And she suspected he enjoyed doing it. He was totally ruthless.

Luisa straightened in her seat and helped herself to scrambled eggs. Well, he could try these tactics on her if he liked. She wasn't afraid of him. In fact, to her own surprise, she found she rather relished the prospect of tangling with him. Tangling in a strictly verbal sense, of course!

'So. I'm waiting.' He was pouring himself more coffee. 'Or would you prefer to leave your confession until you've eaten breakfast?'

Luisa reached for the crispy bacon and added a couple of rashers to her eggs. 'It's all the same to me.' She glanced across at him. 'You're the one who's more likely to have his appetite ruined.'

'Then it's as well that I've finished eating.' He leaned back arrogantly in his chair, clearly contemptuous of her suggestion. 'Frankly, I can't wait to hear what you're going to come up with.'

Luisa took a mouthful of bacon and eggs, chewed unhurriedly, then swallowed. 'How about home-wrecking?' she shot across at him. 'Does that sound like your sort of thing?'

'Home-wrecking?' Roth frowned at her. 'No, I can't say it does.' But there was a fleeting tell-tale flicker at the back of his eyes. 'I'm afraid I must insist that you explain.'

Luisa felt a sudden sharp surge of anger inside her. He knew precisely what she was talking about and he knew also that he was guilty. This show of innocence was shameless deceit!

She laid down her fork and leaned towards him. 'I think home-wrecking is the term that's generally applied when a man, quite simply for the thrill of the conquest, seduces a married woman into abandoning her husband and children. And that's what you are, Mr Elman. A home-wrecker.'

Again, there was that flicker at the back of the dark eyes. Oh, yes, he knew precisely what she was talking about!

Still, it would appear he was a long way from confessing. 'And whose home precisely are you accusing me of wrecking?'

Luisa looked back at him impatiently. 'I think you already know that. Unless, of course,' she added bitingly, 'you have more than one married woman in your life.' Which would not surprise me in the slightest, she added silently.

Roth Elman took another mouthful of his coffee. 'I was not aware that I had any,' he answered calmly.

'Weren't you? Are you really trying to tell me that you didn't know that my sister Rita is married?' She laughed tightly, scornfully. 'I find that extraordinary, considering you've been to her home and met her husband and children!'

There was a moment of silence. Black eyes lifted curiously. Then Roth Elman laughed softly. 'You're Rita's sister?'

Just for a moment Luisa could not speak as a wave of anger and outrage poured through her. Last weekend she'd been at her sister's home in Yorkshire, comforting Alan, the abandoned husband, suddenly forced to contemplate with fear and sadness the future of her now motherless niece and nephew. And now, here she was, looking into the face of the man who was responsible for this human tragedy. And what was he doing? He was laughing.

It was an effort not to throw her bacon and eggs at him. 'I'm glad you think it's funny!' she hissed at him across the table. 'I can assure you that Rita's husband and children don't share the joke!'

His expression had grown more sober, though it still lacked any trace of sympathy. His eyes scanned her face. 'Are you really Rita's sister?'

'Yes, I'm really Rita's sister. Why do you find that so surprising?'

'You're not the least bit like her. There's no resemblance whatsoever. And she's never mentioned to me that she has a sister.'

'Well, she does and it's me. You can take my word for it. Rita Browning is my sister.'

'I would never have guessed it.' Roth sat back in his chair and proceeded to study her with an air of detachment. 'She's so dark and you're so fair. You're so slim... and you're taller...' His eyes narrowed. 'Though perhaps there is a small resemblance. The shape of the nose is not dissimilar. And something about the line of the jaw.'

Then he added, still watching her in that clinically detached fashion, 'You're a lot younger, aren't you? That's what threw me. You can't be any more than twenty-five or twenty-six.'

'You're right, I'm twenty-six, eleven years younger than Rita. And you're also right that we don't look alike—apart from vague similarities around the nose and jawline,' she added with a dash of sarcasm.

At least, she was thinking, he wasn't trying to deny that he was well acquainted with Rita's physiognomy! In fact, he wasn't denying anything!

Sheer arrogance, she decided. Nothing to do with honesty.

She sat back in her seat. 'So, now that we've sorted that out, perhaps you would be good enough to tell me where she is?'

'Tell you where Rita is?' He smiled across at her cynically. 'Surely you already know where she is.'

'No, I don't know where she is. I thought she was with you. It was because I thought she was on the yacht that I gatecrashed the party.'

'And is she?' The dark eyes watched her with amusement. 'Is your sister on board the yacht?'

'I really don't know. I thought I saw her last night. Just a glimpse. But I couldn't be certain. I was looking for her when you found me in the cabin.'

'I see. You were looking for your sister. Now, that's an explanation that hadn't occurred to me.' He smiled a scathing smile, clearly disbelieving, took a bite of his waffle and chewed on it slowly. 'Somehow you didn't look like someone who was looking for her sister.'

'And what is that supposed to mean?' Luisa sat back and fixed her gaze on him. 'How ought I to have looked in your opinion?'

'A little less suspicious. A little less secretive.' He polished off the remains of his waffle. 'If you really were searching for your sister, why didn't you just come and ask me where she was?'

Luisa felt herself blush. Yes, she had acted suspiciously, and in a manner that was totally alien to her nature. She told him, 'Originally, I was planning to come and ask you. Or rather, originally I didn't think that would be necessary. When I came on board, I was expecting to find her with you. I didn't think there'd be any need to have to look for her.

'But then...' She paused, trying to sort out in her mind the confused events of the previous night. 'I thought I saw her—wearing a blue dress—standing in a huddle with you and another couple. But then she seemed to disappear... I searched every corner of the party... but I couldn't find her...'

'So, why didn't you come to me? Surely I was the person most likely to know her whereabouts.'

'I told you, I was going to...'

'Yes, but you didn't.' Dark eyebrows lifted questioningly. 'I'm asking you why?'

Luisa hesitated for a moment, then decided to tell the truth. 'I didn't approach you,' she told him, watching him closely, 'because I suddenly had the feeling that something funny was going on.'

His expression was unfathomable. 'Something funny? What kind of funny?'

'I don't know exactly. Something felt wrong.'

'Explain yourself more clearly. What felt wrong?'

'I can't be more specific. It was just a feeling.' Luisa narrowed her eyes at him and added quickly, before he could intervene again, 'Was I right? Is something going on?'

'Like what, for example?'

'I don't know. You tell me.'

'I have nothing to tell you. I have no idea what you're getting at.'

Luisa sighed. She wasn't really sure what she was getting at either—but it was that feeling that something was not quite right that had triggered her decision to have a quiet little snoop before finally confronting him about Rita last night.

But she was getting nowhere with that line of questioning. She returned to her original query. 'Do you know where my sister is?'

'You mean at this precise moment? No, I'm afraid I can't help you. Somewhere on Nassau, more than likely. But where she's not, I can promise you, is on board this yacht.'

'Was she here last night?'

'Didn't you tell me you saw her?'

'I told you I *thought* I saw her. I wasn't absolutely certain.'

'How could you not be certain?' His tone was scornful. 'Don't you know what your sister looks like?'

Luisa pursed her lips. Arguing with Roth Elman was like trying to climb a mountain of loose shale.

One step forward and two steps back. The more one struggled, the less progress one made!

'Of course I know what my sister looks like!' Luisa took a deep breath. 'But she's lost weight since I last saw her, and changed her hairstyle, and I only caught a fleeting glimpse of her—or someone I thought was her...'

One dark eyebrow lifted. He surveyed her for a moment. 'I get the impression it's a while since you last saw your sister...?'

'Yes, it is. Six months. I haven't seen her since Christmas.'

She was about to add that there was nothing strange about that, that she and Rita had never been particularly close—partly because of the age-gap between them and partly because they lived at opposite ends of the country—but that they kept in regular touch by telephone.

But she stopped herself in time. What was she thinking of? Why on earth should she feel the need to justify herself to Roth Elman?

As he looked back at her, he turned slightly and stretched his long legs out in front of him, the white linen of his trousers tautening against his thighs. Luisa found herself thinking, most inappropriately, that he had the spectacular strong thighs of a highly tuned athlete. It was quite shocking the way that thought tweaked momentarily at her innards.

Then he spoke. 'So, why this sudden anxiety to find your sister?'

'Very simple. I want to try and talk some sense into her and make her see what an absolute fool she's being. I want to persuade her to go back to her family, where she belongs.'

'How very worthy of you.' His tone was cutting. He clearly didn't consider her worthy in the slightest.

'I'm doing it for the sake of her two children. Ronnie and Abigail need their mother.' Luisa looked into his face, searching for some sign of guilt, but of that particular emotion there was not even a glimmer. Irritably, she challenged him. 'Wouldn't you agree that she ought to be with her family?'

Roth did not answer her and it was impossible to tell what was going through his head. He sat back in his seat, crossing his legs at the ankles, and proceeded to examine her minutely for a moment. His expression, if anything, was one of censure.

Luisa shifted in her seat, oddly discomfited, feeling hemmed in by that long, glorious stretch of white-clad leg. She cleared her throat. 'Surely you must agree?' she insisted.

He continued to regard her across the table in silence. Then, narrowing his eyes at her, he demanded, 'What business are your sister's affairs of yours? Wouldn't you say she's old enough to run her own life?'

More than old enough! There was no denying that. Which was why Luisa, at first, had been reluctant to interfere. But she told him now what she had told herself, 'Normally, I would agree. But the circumstances are not normal. My sister has quite clearly taken leave of her sanity.'

'Why so?'

'I'd say the answer to that is obvious. For one thing, she's gone running off with you. And——'

'And you think no woman in her right mind would consider such a thing?'

'I wasn't about to say that.' To Luisa's horror, she blushed. Then she simply increased her own embarrassment by adding hurriedly, 'I suppose there must be many women who would consider such a thing. After all, you're a most attractive man...' She broke off, annoyed at herself. 'You know what I mean.'

Adding to her annoyance, Roth laughed at that, throwing back his head, displaying perfect teeth. Then he held her gaze. 'And you're a most attractive young woman.' His eyes danced across at her. 'You know what I mean.'

Luisa's cheeks were still flaming like Olympic torches. As she met the dark eyes, she could feel ripples rushing through her. Wicked little ripples of excitement.

Shame on you, Luisa Baker! she chided herself guiltily. This despicable man is your sister's lover!

She pulled herself together, staring at the table. 'My sister is a devoted wife and mother,' she told him. 'She'd never have abandoned her children if she'd been in possession of her faculties.'

There followed another silence. Luisa could feel his eyes on her. Then he said, 'I can tell you're one of those busybody types. The type who's forever trying to tell others how to run their lives.'

Luisa snapped her eyes up to look at him. 'Nonsense! I'm not!' Yet, all the same, the accusation struck a chord in her. She did have a habit of becoming involved in other people's problems. But only because they came to her for help and she invariably found it impossible to say no!

She recalled how she'd been drawn into this current private drama.

First, the frantic phone call from her brother-in-law, Alan, the overnight train journey from London to Yorkshire, then the emotional two days they'd spent together, when Alan's desperate tearful pleading had finally convinced her she had to do something.

'You're going to the States, anyway, on business,' he'd argued. 'It wouldn't cost you much to take a quick detour to Nassau. And you're the only one who can help. The way she's feeling right now, totally head over heels with that man, there's not a hope that she'd listen to me.'

That was probably true, but would Rita listen to her either? Luisa had still been reluctant to interfere. What if all that happened when she went to Nassau was that she simply made Rita angry and the situation worse?

Though things could scarcely be worse, she'd found herself thinking as Alan had proceeded to play on her soft spot.

'Think of Ronnie and Abigail, Luisa. Right now, they're safe in France on holiday. They don't even know what's going on. But in three weeks' time their holiday will be over, and what are they going to do without their mother? Think of them, Luisa. Do it for them.'

How could she say no? An image had passed through her head of the last time she had seen the ten-year-old twins with their mother. It seemed impossible to believe that that picture of devotion was in danger of being destroyed forever. For she had always believed that in all the wide world there was no more devoted mother than Rita.

This runaway romance with Roth Elman, she'd decided then, must have been triggered by some crazy kind of brainstorm. Rita would never take the risk of losing her children. It had always been obvious that they meant the world to her.

So she'd said yes to Alan's pleas, cancelled her planned holiday in New Orleans and arranged to fly south to Nassau instead as soon as her business in New York was finished. She'd wished she hadn't had to, but what else could she do?

Roth Elman was watching her across the table now, an amused, uncaring smile on his face. 'So, what do you plan to tell your sister when you see her?'

Luisa decided to pull no punches. She looked straight back at him. 'I plan to tell her that a cheap little fling with you isn't worth losing her family for.'

He laughed at that. 'What makes you think it's a cheap little fling? What makes you think it isn't true love?'

It was Luisa's turn to laugh now, though she felt more sadness than amusement at the cynical, mocking tone that had accompanied that remark.

'Oh, I know it's not true love. At least not on your side.' She glanced away, remembering the letters Alan had shown her, the letters Rita had sent him, full of anguish and ecstasy, telling of her total love for Roth Elman. They were so full of emotion that it had been painful to read them. There was no doubt they'd been written by a woman obsessed.

Another dart of pain went through her now as she looked into Roth's uncaring face. Before she'd even met him she'd sensed in her heart that this love-affair of Rita's was a one-sided thing. To be brutally realistic, men like Roth Elman did not fall in love with women like Rita. If they fell in love at all—and she frankly found that doubtful—they would fall in love with glamorous, worldly women, the type of woman much in evidence at last night's party.

And Rita, for all her prettiness, did not belong in that category, no more than did Luisa herself. Luisa felt her heart go out to her. She was fooling herself.

The arrogant smile on Roth's face confirmed what she was thinking. He didn't need to add, with a callous flash of his dark eyes, 'So, what's wrong with a harmless little fling?'

'For people like you, nothing, I suppose. I imagine flings are the sort of thing you go in for.'

He neither confirmed nor denied that. He simply smiled across at her. 'And you, little sister? How do you feel about flings?'

It was outrageous the way her skin prickled at that remark, but the lazy, sensuous tone in which he'd delivered it had made it sound almost like an invitation. An invitation that, to her horror, had made her breath catch. Once again, she'd felt a little ripple of excitement.

She snapped herself to instantly. 'I don't have flings.'

'Why on earth not? Flings can be fun.'

Again her breath caught. It was the way he was looking at her, running those black-as-midnight eyes over her. It was the way she was aware of the powerful physicality of him. She drew back in her seat, impatient at herself, and understanding even more clearly what had happened to her sister. It would be all too easy, she was starting to realise, to fall prey to the sensuous powers of this man.

She said, 'I'm only interested in serious relationships.'

'Relationships. Plural. Does that mean, as I think it does, that there's no special long-term man in your life?'

How had he figured that out? He was far too clever. Luisa narrowed her eyes at him. 'It's really none of your business, but yes, as a matter of fact, it does.'

'So, what are you doing wrong? You must be doing something wrong. After all, as I've already told you, you're an attractive young woman. I can't imagine you're short of suitors. Yet, in spite of that, and though you take your relationships seriously, here you are alone, without a man in your life.'

He made it sound like a tragedy! Luisa shot him a cool look. 'And who said I need one?' she answered levelly. 'As it happens, I'm doing very well without a man in my life.'

It was true, but all the same she felt needled by his insight. For he was right; when it came to men, she did a lot wrong. For starters, unfailingly, she chose the wrong ones! She thought of Anthony, her last boyfriend. He had definitely been wrong.

'So, it would appear you're not like your sister in this area either.' Roth was eyeing her with impudent amusement. 'Unlike you, your sister doesn't like to be without a man. That is something I can vouch for.'

Luisa felt jolted by the insult. How dare you? she wanted to snap at him. But the protest would have sounded a little hollow. There was every evidence, after all, that what he said was true!

'Nor, unlike you, does she have any objections to a harmless little fling.'

'Perhaps she wasn't aware that was all she was getting—a ''harmless little fling'', as you call it!' Luisa glared at him as she shot the angry riposte at him. 'Not that it would occur to me to describe as harmless something that breaks up a once happy family!'

As Roth simply looked back at her without a gram of remorse, she challenged him, 'Why did you mess with my sister? You knew from the start that she was married!'

'As presumably she did also.' His gaze was steady, unrepentant. 'Anything your sister did, she did freely, because she wanted to. At no point, I can assure you, did I force her at gunpoint.'

It was at that moment that a crew member appeared at Roth's elbow. 'A phone call from Houston, sir. Do you wish to take it here?'

'No, I'll take it in my office.' Roth rose to his feet unhurriedly, his eyes never leaving Luisa's flushed face. 'You're wasting your time here. Your sister's not on board. Feel free to search the yacht, if you like.'

He tossed down his napkin. 'But, if you're really anxious to see her, I suggest you go and look elsewhere.' He paused. 'If you like, you can hitch a lift back to Nassau. There'll be a helicopter stopping by to pick up some stuff for me in half an hour. Let me know if you want to go on it.'

He smiled a grim smile. 'Perhaps I also ought to point out that it'll be your last chance to get back to Nassau for several days.'

Luisa watched him go with a sense of frustration. Reluctantly, she believed his claim that Rita wasn't here. In which case, he was right, there was no point in her staying.

She poured herself some coffee. Perhaps they'd fallen out. Perhaps that was why her sister wasn't on the yacht. She felt a spurt of hope. Perhaps Rita was back in England. Perhaps this whole unhappy mess had already sorted itself out.

But she couldn't believe that. Remembering Rita's letters, remembering the almost frantic intensity of emotion that had seemed to jump from every line, she couldn't believe that, even in the face of a tiff, her sister would just pack up and go meekly home. She had to be somewhere here in the Bahamas.

And I have to find her. Luisa stared out at the horizon, a pencil line drawn between two vivid shades of blue. So, it seemed the wisest thing she could do was return to Nassau and continue her search there.

At that moment a steward appeared with a pot of fresh coffee. Luisa turned to him, her mind made up. 'Kindly let Mr Elman know that I'll be taking the helicopter back to Nassau.'

Half an hour later, she was ready and waiting on deck, her green silk evening gown and purse and shoes neatly wrapped up in a brown paper parcel, as the helicopter at last came into view. There was no sign of Roth, for which she was thankful. It would be her pleasure just to leave and never set eyes on him again.

The helicopter landed, creating a noisy mini whirlwind, and almost at once Luisa was being helped aboard and buckled into her seat as the pilot told her, 'Just make yourself comfortable. I won't be a minute.'

Then she was watching as he jumped down on to the deck and hurried to the far end where Roth had suddenly appeared. She glared at Roth. Good riddance! she was thinking.

But then, suddenly, unexpectedly, he raised his head and glanced across at her. And there was just something about him, about the way he was smiling, that caused a spark of doubt to ignite in her heart.

Was she doing the right thing? He looked too pleased to see the back of her. Maybe she had made the wrong decision, after all?

In an instant, she made her mind up, as she saw the pilot turn around and start to make his way back towards the helicopter. She unbuckled her belt and scrambled to the ground, just as he swung himself back on board.

'I'm not coming, but take the parcel, please, the one by my seat, and deliver it by cab to the address that's written on it.' She reached into her pocket and drew out her twenty-dollar bill. 'This ought to cover it,' she added, thrusting it into his hand.

Then, ignoring his puzzled look, she was hurrying across the deck, noticing that there was no longer any sign of Roth. Good! she thought. At least he can't stop me! For suddenly she was filled with the total certainty that the only way to find Rita was by sticking with Roth. A decision, she sensed, of which he would definitely not approve!

It was a good couple of minutes later when he reappeared, as sudden as a leopard's cough, right in front of her.

He smiled into her face. 'So, you're staying, after all? Good. I couldn't have planned things better.'

Then he was turning on his heel with one last triumphant glance at her, as, with a shiver of horror, Luisa realised what had happened.

He had double tricked her into staying. He had never wanted her to leave. And she, fool that she was, had fallen hook, line and sinker!

With a start of sudden panic she swung round towards the helicopter. 'Stop!' she yelled. 'Wait for me!'

But the helicopter, her last hope of returning to Nassau, was already lifting up into the sky and swinging away.

CHAPTER THREE

AS THE helicopter soared off, turning into a speck in the blue sky, Luisa watched it with a sense of sudden sharp uneasiness. Roth had wanted her to stay, though for what reason she couldn't fathom. And while appearing to assist her to do the very opposite, he had somehow manipulated her into doing as he desired.

Feeling suddenly, eerily, at his mercy, Luisa stood for a while staring out at the ocean, glittering like crushed blue ice in the sun, and tried to shake off this feeling that she was somehow Roth's hostage. The decision not to leave had been *hers*, not Roth Elman's, and she had made it for a perfectly rational reason!

Well, perhaps not rational, she acknowledged more honestly. She had made it on the strength of an intuition. But it had been *her* intuition. No one had planted it!

And even now, through her uneasiness, she still stood by that intuition. The only way she was going to find her sister was through Roth, she was sure of it. Voluntarily or involuntarily, he would eventually lead the way.

Luisa leaned against the guard rail, feeling the wind in her hair, breathing in deeply the clean salt air, and tried to sort out the questions that were streaming through her head.

Why would Roth trick her into staying? Surely, she told herself, that made no sense? More likely, he would have been glad to see the back of her!

Yet, if that was the case, why hadn't he forced her to leave—simply bundled her bodily on to the helicopter? He could easily have done that. But he hadn't.

Luisa bit her lip and frowned at the horizon. There was no point in asking herself all these questions. If she wanted answers, it was Roth she had to ask.

She turned round determinedly, her eyes scanning the fore deck. There was no sign of him any more, but he couldn't have gone far. She thrust her hands into her shorts pockets and marched towards the helm. She would dig him out and demand some explanations!

'Mr Elman is busy. He can't be disturbed. However, I'll let him know that you wish to see him.'

Luisa suppressed a grimace. That was the response she'd been expecting. Everyone she asked gave her the same answer. The captain, Roth's personal secretary and now his personal steward, whom she'd finally managed to track down in the linen room.

'Would you tell him, please, that I wish to see him urgently?' She suppressed her irritation. It wasn't the poor steward's fault. 'And remind him that I've been trying to see him all day.'

'I will do, Miss Baker.' The steward nodded, as he lifted down an armful of green towels from a shelf. 'Don't worry, I'll be sure to pass on your message.'

'Thanks. I'd be most grateful.'

Luisa was about to move away, but suddenly, inadvertently, her attention was caught by the legend on the border of one of the big green towels.

'Gymnasium', it said in bold yellow letters.

And suddenly, in a flash of inspiration, Luisa knew precisely where Roth was keeping himself so busy! In the on-board gymnasium, that was where he was! And his steward, unless she was badly mistaken, was on his way there now with a fresh supply of towels!

She turned away, as though going about her business, but then ducked back into a doorway and waited there, hidden, until she heard the door of the linen room click shut and observed the steward setting off along the gangway. Keeping out of sight, discreetly, she followed him.

The gymnasium, she discovered, was up on the top sun deck. As the steward disappeared inside, Luisa hid round a corner, then waited ten minutes until he re-emerged and, whistling to himself, went back down to the lower deck. She took a deep breath. The way was now clear for her to beard the lion in his den!

It was quite a gym. Luisa stood in the doorway and gazed round for a moment at the array of state-of-the-art equipment suspended from the ceiling, projecting from the walls and laid out dauntingly over the polished wooden floor. This was definitely no place for wimps!

But it was not the exceptional hardware that really caught and held her eye. What drew her attention like a magnet drew metal was the figure in the body-hugging shorts and vest, currently lying on his back, feet on the floor, lifting between clenched fists a heavy bar of metal that to Luisa looked as though it might once have been part of the yacht. How could anyone lift a chunk of steel that size?

'So, you tracked me down?'

As he spoke, Luisa jumped. Anyone engaged in such demanding physical exercise she had assumed would be incapable of speech. To her annoyance Roth didn't even sound out of breath!

She stepped towards him, intensely aware of his semi-nakedness, and came to a stop a couple of metres away. 'I wanted to talk to you,' she said.

'About what?'

Without glancing at her, he continued to pump the heavy weight, lowering it to his chest, then straightening his arms again to lift it high above his head. Luisa watched him, mesmerised by the sight of rippling muscles.

She said, 'I wanted to ask you why you want to keep me here.'

He did glance at her then, dark eyes flashing amusedly. 'Shouldn't that question be the other way round?' he put to her. 'Shouldn't *I* be asking *you* why you decided to stay?'

'I stayed because I'm sure you know where Rita is and because one way or another I plan to get you to tell me.' She paused and took another, wary step closer. 'But what I can't understand is why you want me to stay.'

'Who said I did?' He flicked another quick glance at her as he continued to pump the steel bar up and down. 'What makes you think I want you to stay?'

'Because you allowed me to.'

Her gaze flickered over him, over the broad muscular chest, beaded now with sweat, over the smooth bulging shoulders, electric with power, over the sinewy arms, the long muscle-packed legs. The vest he wore clung to him like a second skin, a second skin he seemed about to burst out of at any moment, and the tight shorts moulded every splendid virile contour.

A man like him, with a physique like his, she found herself thinking with a twist of sinful pleasure, how could she have fought him if he'd wanted her to leave? He could make her do anything he wanted!

Not quite! She checked herself and the shiver that had gone through her. His powers did not extend quite that far!

She elaborated, swallowing and returning her gaze to his face, 'You wouldn't have allowed me to stay unless you'd wanted me to. I think I know you well enough to safely assume that.'

'So, you feel you're getting to know me, do you?'

'A little. Reluctantly.'

Roth smiled. 'So, you tell me why I would want you to stay.'

'I can't begin to imagine. Why don't *you* tell *me*?'

He continued to breathe deeply, pumping the steel bar rhythmically. 'Have I given you the impression of being desperate for your company?'

'Oh, definitely not.' Luisa laughed at that. 'Whatever reason you have, that's definitely not it.'

'Then what is, I wonder?'

Abruptly, taking her by surprise, he'd laid the bar down on the bar rest behind his head and had risen to his feet to stand beside her. 'A smart girl like you,' he said, 'you must have worked something out.'

Luisa had taken a step back, her heart flying to her mouth. Suddenly all that hot, raw masculinity was standing before her, only inches away. She felt a quiver go through her. Her stomach twisted strangely. She had a sudden fierce urge to reach out and touch him.

She said with difficulty, for her throat had gone quite dry, 'How can I know what reasons you have?'

Roth reached for a towel that lay on a stool by the weight machine. He rubbed his damp hair. 'You must have thought about it,' he said.

'I have, but since I can't see inside your head the only way I can know is if you tell me.'

'You surprise me.' Roth rubbed the back of his neck. His dark hair, Luisa observed, which clung damply to his scalp was now raised where he had rubbed it in untidy little tufts. It was an effort not to reach out her hand and smooth it.

She swallowed again. Was she going crazy? She focused on his face. 'In what way do I surprise you?'

'You're a journalist, aren't you?' He tossed the towel back on the stool. 'I thought journalists were experts at reaching conclusions out of nothing.'

Luisa pulled a face. That comment was predictable. Roth never had a good word to say about the Press. But she resisted the urge to defend her profession—now was not the time to get into a discussion about that!—and said instead, observing as she did so that the green towel had slipped from the stool to the floor, 'What's the matter? Why can't you just tell me why you want to keep me here?' Automatically, she bent forward to pick the towel up.

That was when he surprised her. He reached forward suddenly and caught her swiftly by the wrist. 'Leave it,' he told her. 'Leave it where it is. I don't need you or anyone else picking up after me.'

'But——'

'But nothing!' He snatched the towel from her and very deliberately dropped it back on the floor. 'I can't bear women who try to organise me.'

'But I wasn't trying to...'

Luisa's protest trailed off. Suddenly all thoughts of what had prompted her action had vanished completely from her head. All she could think of was the vibrant male physique that was suddenly so close that it seemed to swallow her up. She hated the way she rather liked the feeling. It was a feeling that was new to her and strangely exciting.

Shame on you! She wrestled to pull her wrist free, her eyes sparking with hastily summoned indignation. 'Let me go! What the devil do you think you're doing?'

He released her. 'No need to panic.' The dark eyes were amused now. 'Do you always get in such a state whenever a man touches you?'

'That wasn't touching, that was grabbing.' Luisa glared at him. 'And I'm not in the habit of being grabbed.'

'No, I don't suppose you are.' He was smiling a taunting smile at her. 'Those young men of yours, with whom you have these serious relationships, I'm sure wouldn't go in for anything so vulgarly physical.'

Luisa found it hard to hold his gaze. He's right, she was thinking, her past relationships could in no way, shape or form be described, even remotely, as vulgarly physical. Quite the opposite, in fact, she reflected with a small sigh. They had all been most tasteful and inclined towards the cerebral. The physical side of things had barely come into it.

And suddenly she recalled his crude comment about Rita and how, unlike herself, she needed a man. Well, she had certainly found one in Roth Elman! she decided, not at all certain why she felt quite wistful at that thought. Roth Elman was the last man *she* would want in her life!

'So, have you recovered now?' He had moved away from her and was leaning casually against the wall bars. 'Have you recovered from the trauma of being grabbed by some uncouth man?'

He smiled as he said it and Luisa wanted to smile back. The description 'uncouth', she was thinking, was totally misapplied. In spite of his physicality, there was nothing uncouth about Roth. On the contrary, there was a natural elegance and grace about him that was oddly engaging as he leaned there, casually, against the wall bars. It would be very easy to stop being angry with him. Even to entirely forget what type of man he was.

But she forced herself not to smile but to answer tightly, 'Yes, I have.'

Roth was still smiling, watching her beneath his lashes. 'So, in the meantime, have you come up with any theories as to why I supposedly want to keep you here?'

As a matter of fact, she had. And it was thinking of Rita that had done it.

Luisa put to him, 'Perhaps you want to keep me away from Rita, so I can't influence her and break up the affair?'

'Now, that's one theory I hadn't thought of.' The dark eyes held hers. 'Could you really do that? Influence your sister to the extent that she'd abandon a love-affair with me?'

'I'd have a damned good try.'

'Oh, yes, I'm sure you would. As I've already told you, I'm well aware of your interfering nature.' He held her eyes a moment, a smile curving his lips, letting his gaze drift over her unhurriedly. Then, as she started to glance away, oddly disturbed by his warm scrutiny, he added, 'But would your sister listen? That's the question I'm really asking.'

Luisa shook herself inwardly. 'There's a good chance she might.' Then she threw him a steely look. 'Why? Does that worry you?'

'Enough to want to keep you here on the yacht with me, you mean?' He laughed. 'It's time you knew something about my character. When I want something, I take it, and after I've taken it I keep it. I don't let anyone, not even meddling sisters, take it away from me.'

That was plain enough, and Luisa did not doubt the truth of it. But did these feelings apply to Rita? she wondered. Had she been wrong in her assessment that he was only playing with her sister?

She said, looking straight at him, 'Do you love my sister?'

'Who was talking about love?' His gaze never flickered. 'I mentioned wanting and keeping. I never mentioned love.'

Luisa felt a coldness touch her. What he was saying was slightly shocking, though really she should have known not to expect any better of him. It was impossible to imagine Roth Elman loving anyone.

In silence for a moment she watched as he bent down and picked up a small weight from the box at his feet. As he tested it in his hand, his fingers gripping it round its middle, the muscles of his upper arm tensed and rippled.

She removed her eyes from his rippling muscles and conceded, 'Yes, you're right. Love doesn't come into it. For you, taking and keeping is an end in itself, whether we're talking about people or material things.'

He raised one eyebrow curiously. 'Explain yourself,' he said.

'Oh, I don't really think explanations are necessary.' Almost wearily, as though suddenly realising what she was up against, Luisa sank down on to the stool where the towel had briefly lain. 'I think we both know what I'm getting at.'

'You may. I don't.' He tossed the weight from hand to hand, his movements, like his lies, easy and effortless. 'I'm afraid you've lost me. You'll have to explain.'

Luisa shook her head. Such innocence! What an actor! Then she faced him with the truth. 'Don't you think,' she put to him, 'that you've already taken more than enough from my brother-in-law, Alan?'

Roth weighed the weight in his hand as though weighing her question. He tossed her a cool glance. 'I take it you're talking about the company?'

'That's right. My brother-in-law Alan's company.'

'Not any more. The company now belongs to me.' He fixed her with a look that would have cut concrete. 'And before you start accusing me of having come by it improperly, I would remind you that when I took over your brother-in-law's company it was literally on its knees, on the brink of closure. When I took over that company I was doing your brother-in-law a favour.'

Luisa smiled cynically. She remembered all too clearly. And, yes, in the beginning it had seemed he'd done Alan a favour. She remembered her brother-in-law's elation when Elman's huge conglomerate had first expressed interest in taking him over. 'I'm saved!' he'd cheered. 'I'm not going to go bankrupt, after all!'

And neither he had. The take-over had gone ahead. And the company had lived on to make a remarkable recovery.

But in the process Alan had lost both his job and his wife.

Shaking her head, Luisa put to Roth, 'I wouldn't call it a favour to take over someone's company, promise him he can stay on as director, then, three months later, throw him out. That's the kind of favour most people can do without.'

'I had reasons for throwing him out.'

'Yes, I bet you did! You wanted your own man running the show, someone who would agree with whatever you said, someone who would follow your orders without question. You got rid of Alan because he had a mind of his own!'

'Is that what he told you?'

'As a matter of fact it was. Why? Are you suggesting that wasn't the case?'

Roth tossed the weight unhurriedly from one hand to the other. 'I'll admit I wasn't happy with some things he was doing. You could say we didn't exactly see eye to eye.'

'You saw eye to eye with his wife, however, didn't you?' Suddenly indignant at his coolness, Luisa spat the accusation at him. 'You didn't have any problem seeing eye to eye with Rita!'

For that was when it had all started, Alan had told her. Secretly, behind his back, while he'd been under the impression that Roth's continued presence in Yorkshire had been motivated solely by his expressed determination to get the company back on its feet, what had really been going on was the seduction of Alan's wife. Right there on his own doorstep Roth had stolen her from him.

But now, instead of shame at his despicable behaviour, all Luisa could see shining in his dark eyes was arrogance.

With what could only be described as contempt, he said, 'I take it Alan also told you that?'

'Alan told me everything.'

'It would appear so.'

'Right from the start, even while negotiations were going on, even before the take-over was completed, you were messing around with Alan's wife.'

'And she with me, presumably?' He smiled as he said it. 'The messing around you're referring to was surely mutual?'

Luisa looked back at him with censure. 'You have no shame, have you? Didn't you care that she was another man's wife?'

'That was for her to care about, not me. Her husband's her responsibility.'

'And what about her children? Don't you feel responsible for them, either? Don't you care that you've left them without a mother? Don't you care about anything at all—anything other than taking and keeping?'

Her voice had risen on a harsh note and now it broke with emotion. As he just stood there against the wall bars, shifting the weight from hand to hand, with no more sign of remorse in his expression than shone from the cold metal in his fist, Luisa snatched a steadying breath and demanded,

'Why did you do it? You admit you don't love her. Was it just for the hell of it or what?'

Roth said nothing for a moment. His features were stony. 'Perhaps the question you should really be asking is why did *she* do it. She's the one with a marriage and children.'

'But it's obvious why she did it!' Luisa's eyes scanned his tall figure, perhaps a little more admiringly than she'd intended. Deliberately, she quenched her admiration and looked him in the eye.

'My sister's a housewife. She leads an unexciting life. A worthwhile life, but an unexciting one. Someone like you, well-known, with your kind of lifestyle—yachts in the Bahamas, snappy clothes, Rolls-Royces—it couldn't have been too difficult for you to sweep her off her feet. In fact, I can imagine it wasn't difficult at all.' She paused. 'I can understand why my sister did it.'

'You flatter me.'

'I don't intend to.'

'Nevertheless, I'm flattered.' Roth smiled. 'But you really must stop paying me all those compliments. I'll start to get the idea you like me.'

'That would be a big mistake.' But she blushed as she said it—though heaven knew why, there was no danger of her *liking* him!

He caught her blush and let his smile grow even wider. 'You look very pretty when your cheeks go all pink. Kind of innocent and childlike. Very appealing.' Then, to her astonishment, he reached out and touched one pink cheek with his finger. 'Not at all like Rita. I've never seen her blush.'

His finger seemed to hover there, softly, against her skin, as his eyes looked down at her, a sudden warmth in their depths.

'No,' he said again. 'Not at all like Rita.'

Luisa's heart was fluttering strangely, like tiny wings beating, nervously, excitedly, inside her breast. She looked back at him helplessly, mesmerised by the touch of him, drawn by that seductive look of warmth.

Then a voice spoke inside her, the voice of reproval. This is your sister's lover, it reminded her sharply, and he's playing games with you just as he's been doing with her.

That thought sobered her up. She jerked away from him. 'I'm Rita's sister, and that tie goes very deep. So, don't make the mistake of thinking otherwise. My sister's interests are mine as well.'

Roth's hand still hovered in the air between them, but as he looked at her all the warmth had gone out of his eyes. 'Yes, of course,' he said. His tone was clipped. Then he bent down and dropped the steel weight back in its box. 'If you don't mind,' he added, straightening, 'I think I'll go and take a shower now.'

Luisa took a deep breath and rose to her feet. She felt oddly deflated by the passing of that warm moment. But she forced her mind to focus on her mission.

'Won't you tell me where she is?' She addressed his broad back as Roth headed across the gym towards the changing-rooms. 'You don't really want her. Let me go to her. Let me persuade her to go home to her husband and family.'

He ignored her totally. He just kept on walking.

Luisa hurried after him, suddenly possessed of a fierce need to have this whole business over and done with.

'Please! Have some feeling. Think of her children. Tell me where she is. It'll be best for everyone.'

'Don't you listen when I speak?' He had turned round so violently that Luisa skidded and almost fell in an effort not to collide with him. His eyes blazed down at her with barely contained anger. 'Don't pester me! I already told you I don't know where she is!'

'But you must have some idea!' He had turned and was striding off again. 'I can't believe,' Luisa pleaded, 'that you have no idea at all!'

He had reached the door of the changing-room. With the flat of his hand, he pushed it open. 'The subject is closed. I don't wish to discuss it!'

But Luisa could not let go. 'What's the matter? Have you fallen out with her? Is that why you don't know where she is?'

It was as though he hadn't heard her. As she demanded again, 'Is it?' Roth stepped through the open doorway and the door swung shut behind him.

For one angry moment Luisa stood glaring at the door. How dared he treat her with such contempt? She had a right to ask him the questions she was asking, and he had a responsibility to answer them!

Filled with fury, Luisa strode towards the door. 'I asked you a question——!' she began, pushing it open. But then she stopped dead in her tracks.

He was a fast undresser, she observed, her colour rising. His vest already lay discarded on the floor and he was in the process of peeling off his shorts.

'Well, well!' He turned to look at her as she froze in the doorway. 'What a nice surprise. You've come to join me in the shower.'

'No, I haven't. I've come to get an answer to my question!'

She'd been in half a mind to dive back out of the door again. But there was little point in that now. She'd seen all there was to see. Before he'd finished speaking, his shorts were on the floor—and goodness, thought Luisa, he was well constructed! Unhurriedly now, he was tying a green towel around his waist.

He regarded her narrowly. 'I told you the subject is closed.'

'Just because you say so? I'm afraid I can't accept that!'

To her annoyance, in response he turned and headed for the showers.

'All I want is for you to tell me where my sister is. Or, if you don't know precisely, to tell me where she might be.' She glared at his retreating back. 'Why won't you tell me?'

Still ignoring her, he stepped into the big tiled shower-room. Her demands mattered less to him than the dust in the air.

Luisa knew that she really ought just to leave it, that she would get nothing out of him while he was in this mood. But suddenly she was eaten up with frustration and anger. On stiff, outraged legs, she followed him through to the shower-room.

'Just answer my question. That's all I ask!'

He was leaning towards the taps, switching on the water. As she came up behind him, the air was filled with spraying water. Roth turned round to face her. 'I told you, the subject's closed.' One hand moved pointedly to the towel at his waist. 'And now I'm going to take a shower.'

Her gaze followed his hand. 'You won't intimidate me with that.' And even to her own ears it sounded an odd choice of words.

She saw amusement touch his eyes. She took a hopeful step forward. 'Look, please,' she began, her tone softer, more pleading. But that was when her foot suddenly slipped on the wet tiles.

Before she could fall, Roth had caught hold of her, firmly, but, as he did so, foolishly Luisa tried to pull away. And, suddenly, in her rubber flip-flops, she was slithering hopelessly, jerking away from him as he tried to haul her upright, her arms and legs flying in every direction.

'Keep still! Do you want to hurt yourself, you idiot?'

At last he had snatched her upright. He held her firmly. 'I'm getting a little tired of you and your silly games!'

'You're the one who's playing games!' She was virtually beneath the shower. She could feel the cold water splashing against her back.

'Oh, no, *you*'re the one who's playing games! This whole damned thing's a silly game!' Suddenly, he shook her, his anger springing from his face. 'And I've had enough of your games! I've had enough of all this nonsense! What kind of idiot do you take me for?'

'I don't know what you're talking about!'

Luisa tried to pull away from him, but there was nowhere to go, except further into the shower. He was blocking her path back into the room.

'So, you want to take a shower, after all, I see...'

As she stepped back, he held her there, right under the jets of water, so that suddenly it was pouring over her, drenching her to the skin. And without mercy his eyes continued to flay her.

'Let's stop this stupid game. Let's stop it right this minute. Let's stop pretending that the reason you're here is in order to save your sister from my clutches. We both know that's a lie and the game's gone on long enough.'

'I don't know what you're talking about!' Luisa spluttered incoherently. And she didn't. All at once he was talking in riddles. She gulped for air. 'Let me out of here! I'm drowning!'

But he did not release her. He thrust his face closer. 'We both know the real reason why you're here—and the real reason why you decided to stay!'

'Do we?'

'Yes, we do.'

'Well, I don't! You'll have to tell me.'

'Stop lying, Luisa!'

'I'm not lying! I swear it!'

As he shook her again, Luisa's heart was beating strangely. Beneath the outward anger she had the odd sensation that something dangerously intimate was passing between them. For a moment, as she looked into his smoky dark eyes, whose expression, she noted, had subtly altered, she was aware of the water pouring between them, bouncing against their bodies, seeming to unite them in a private, misty, wet little world. And from the way his eyes glinted she could sense he sensed it, too.

And for an instant all the antagonism seemed to melt away from them. As their eyes locked and held, Luisa once again was filled with a painful, almost irresistible longing to reach out and touch this unsettling, dark-eyed man.

But that was when he released her, stepping away as he did so.

'Get out of here!' he growled. 'Before I get really angry. Before I drown you for real, the way you deserve, you nasty, grubby little muck-raking spy!'

Luisa did not wait for a second invitation, nor to ask him what he'd meant by that furious accusation. Before he could change his mind, she was diving from the shower and skidding across the tiled floor towards the changing-room, her heart in turmoil, her soul in a state of panic.

Though her turmoil and panic, she realised dimly, had nothing whatsoever to do with his anger. They had been stirred by something else entirely. Something inside herself. Something deep and hidden.

Or something that once had been deep and hidden, but now was rising up like a wall of flames inside her.

CHAPTER FOUR

BACK in her cabin Luisa sat on her bunk bed, wrapped in the towelling robe from the bathroom, and considered what had happened between herself and Roth.

It was scandalous, she told herself. The man was a bully. To have done what he did—to have held her under the shower like that!—well, the only word to describe it was outrageous!

And she was indeed outraged. Yet she couldn't help but ask herself, Why had she followed him into the changing-room in the first place?

She regarded her reflection in the long mirror on the wall. Surely, she told herself, you knew that was asking for trouble? With any other man you might have got away with it. But there was no chance of getting away with it with Roth Elman!

And that was the whole crux of the problem, she told herself. The abominable, contemptible, arrogant Roth Elman was unlike other men, certainly any she'd ever known. And, quite simply, she was at a loss to know how to handle him.

She leaned back against the pillows and crossed her legs at the ankles and tried to picture how Anthony would have behaved today. If, in the heat of an argument, she'd pursued *him* into the changing-room and caught him in a state of near total undress, how would the scenario have developed?

A smile touched Luisa's lips. Dear, sweet Anthony. He and she had been friends for almost a year. Well, more than friends, really. Girlfriend and boyfriend. Though they had never been more than that. They had never been lovers. And in the end, when it had become clear that the relationship was going nowhere, she'd been glad for him when he'd met Angela and gone off and got married.

She'd even smiled when he'd told her, 'I really owe it all to you. If you hadn't persuaded me to take that job in Doncaster I would never have met Angela in the first place.'

'You see, I told you,' she'd answered, giving him a peck on the cheek. 'I told you that if you went lots of good things would come out of it.' She'd smiled into his blue eyes. 'I hope you'll be happy.'

In her mind's eye Luisa could see those blue eyes now as she imagined how he would have reacted in the changing-room.

The first thing Anthony would have done was apologise, she decided, for having allowed himself to be caught in an improper state of dress. Then he would have approached her gently and urged her to calm down. He might even have slipped a comforting arm round her shoulder. Then, once she'd calmed down, he would have answered her questions. And then he'd have gone off and taken his shower.

What a civilized little scenario. Luisa stared at the ceiling. And what was more, it was how most men of her acquaintance would have acted. Most men of her acquaintance, unlike Roth Elman, were not savages!

She closed her eyes for a moment and relived that scene in the shower—the way he'd held her there and shaken her and thrust his face close to hers, how he'd trapped her with that menacingly muscular body.

He was so damned physical! Everything about him was physical! She wasn't used to such overpowering physicality!

That thought caused her to frown inside her head a moment. Was that why she had reacted to him as she had, with that flickering awareness of a sense of intimacy between them? For that fleeting but vivid instant had she simply been overpowered? Was it not true what she had feared—that he had awakened something within her?

She stood up as there was a sudden tap on the door. The only thing Roth Elman is capable of awakening in me is anger and dislike, she told herself sternly, as she strode across the cabin. I find his behaviour despicable!

It was the steward come to deliver her newly laundered shorts and shirt.

Luisa smiled at the young man. 'That was quick. I'm really grateful.' Then she frowned as he held out to her another plastic-wrapped hanger.

'Mr Elman said you needed a change of clothes, and I'm afraid these were the best we could come up with.' The steward smiled. 'They belong to one of the junior deck-hands. He's the smallest chap on board. They were the only things we thought might fit.'

'That was good of you to take the trouble.' Luisa smiled gratefully as she peeked under the plastic cover to discover immaculately pressed white trousers and a couple of white T-shirts. 'It'll make a change from wearing shorts all the time.'

As he was about to take his leave, the steward paused. 'Oh, I forgot... Mr Elman asked if you would care to join him for dinner? He'll be dining in the main dining-room as usual about half-past eight.'

Will he, indeed? How jolly nice for him! Luisa shook her head politely. 'Please tell him I won't be joining him. I'll dine in my cabin, if it's all the same.'

And as she closed the cabin door, she felt quite hot with irritation. Did he really have the arrogant nerve to suppose she would consider dining with him after the way he'd behaved?

Quite frankly, she decided, I'd sooner starve to death!

In fact, Luisa was not required to starve.

Just after eight, as she sat reading one of the books that she'd discovered on a shelf at the side of the wardrobe, her dinner was delivered to her on a silver tray. A seafood starter, followed by chicken and fresh vegetables, a dish of home-made ice cream and a half-carafe of wine. She polished the lot off gratefully. She'd been hungry and it was delicious.

She was out in the gangway, leaning against the handrail, still dressed in her bath-robe, sipping a glass of wine, when the steward returned to retrieve her tray.

They exchanged a friendly word or two, then Luisa watched him hurry off, reflecting what an extremely pleasant chap he was, when she suddenly caught sight of a figure on the upper deck, standing in the shadows, as though he was watching her.

It wasn't Roth. He wasn't tall enough. And, as she glanced up to see him, the figure darted rather hurriedly out of sight.

How strange, Luisa thought, taking a sip of her wine. What on earth can he be doing?

She took another sip of wine and thought no more about it, then went back into her cabin and read some more of her book. But an hour or so later, feeling in need of a breath of fresh air, she stepped outside again and automatically glanced up.

And again she was aware of a figure stepping back into the shadows. She stared into the darkness. How very odd. And it was only then, in a sudden bright flash of remembrance, that she recalled Roth's angry accusation in the shower-room.

'We both know the real reason why you're here!' he'd accused her. 'You nasty, grubby little muck-raking spy!'

At the time she'd assumed he was speaking spiteful nonsense. There was no other rational explanation. Now suddenly she wondered. Had he been serious? Did he believe she was a spy—and had he appointed someone to spy on *her*?

It was an intolerable thought. It sent shivers through her. This man was adding insult to injury!

Well, she would not have it! She glanced at her watch. It was just after nine-thirty. Maybe he was still eating.

She stepped back into the cabin, slipped off her bath-robe and pulled on the white trousers and one of her new T-shirts.

Then, with a cautious glance at the figure in the shadows, she was striding off with the light of battle in her eyes, along the narrow gangway, towards the main dining-room.

'You're a little late for dinner, but come and join me for a brandy.'

Roth was not in the dining-room. He had already finished eating. But a steward had kindly directed Luisa to the billiard room, where she found him standing at the end of the vast table, unhurriedly chalking the end of his cue.

He gestured towards the array of bottles on a nearby bar table. 'Please don't think me inhospitable if I invite you to help yourself.'

He was dressed in black trousers and a white jacket and shirt. Immaculate, expensive-looking, perfectly cut. And as he laid down the chalk and leaned across the table to take a shot, his raven-dark hair glistened richly beneath the table lights.

Luisa had never seen a man look more beautiful in her life. She was aware of her heart turning over inside her. What a pity, she found herself thinking, that he's such a rotter.

She said, 'I didn't come here for a brandy.'

'I guessed that.' As his shot connected, the ball rolled into the pocket. 'It wouldn't be like you to have something so civil on your mind.'

Hah! That was a joke! 'You should talk about civility! I wouldn't call your behaviour this afternoon civil!'

'And I suppose yours was?' Roth straightened and turned to glance at her, reaching as he did so for the crystal brandy glass that was balanced on the edge of the mahogany billiard table. His eyes glinted wickedly as he took a long, slow mouthful and rolled the brandy in his mouth for a moment before swallowing. 'I suppose you consider it perfectly civil to go around ambushing defenceless naked men in changing-rooms?'

'I didn't ambush you!' Luisa's cheeks had turned crimson. 'And anyway,' she added, feeling on slightly surer ground, 'I would hardly describe you as being in any way defenceless!'

'Just as well I'm not.' He smiled broadly in amusement. 'You can be pretty ferocious when you're aroused.'

Luisa was suddenly finding it hard to keep her gaze steady. It was that word 'aroused' and the way he'd looked at her as he'd said it, making it sound like some sinful sexual promise. She hated the way her flesh had responded.

Then he added, turning more fully to face her, 'So, tell me, did you enjoy your shower?'

'Not a great deal.' Her skin was suddenly prickling with the memory of that moment that had passed between them in the shower-room. Her voice was gruff as she added, 'I thought you had a nerve.'

'You needed cooling down.' The dark eyes danced with amusement. 'I find cold showers can be most effective.'

Luisa grimaced. 'Yes, I suppose you'd know all about that.'

Roth laughed. 'A bit. I've taken my share of cold showers.' Then he nodded his dark head. 'And yours seems to have done the trick. You appear to be in a much more palatable frame of mind.'

As Luisa opened her mouth, about to disabuse him of that notion—it was a far from palatable frame of mind that had brought her here!—Roth held up one hand and warned her quietly, 'I've just had a most enjoyable dinner and am now enjoying a soothing brandy and a game of billiards... so I would ask you most sincerely not to upset my digestion by resuming this afternoon's conversation. I've already had enough of that for one day, thank you.'

Luisa bit her lip. 'OK,' she agreed. 'I won't say a word about my sister.' Then, as he laid down his brandy glass and leaned over the table again, considering the best angle for his next shot, she crossed to the drinks table and poured herself a small sherry. Why not have a drink? After all, she was in no hurry.

She fixed her eyes on his back as she took a mouthful. By the look of things she had two choices. She could forget what she'd come for and just spend a pleasant hour with him, for he did seem to be in an agreeable frame of mind. Or she could stick to her purpose and seriously ruffle his feathers.

It was the attractiveness of that former option that caused her to reject it. The last thing she should feel tempted by was a pleasant hour with Roth Elman!

So she took a deep breath and asked him straight, 'Have you set one of your crew to spy on me?'

Luisa was totally unprepared for his reaction. As another ball dropped neatly into the pocket, Roth turned to glance at her over his shoulder. 'Yes, as a matter of fact, I have,' he answered.

Luisa blinked in surprise. Her eyes widened. 'Why?'

'For the obvious purpose. To keep an eye on you.' He even smiled, not a single glossy feather ruffled. 'I've appointed three crew members—they're to work in eight-hour shifts—to keep you under surveillance at all times.'

'But why?' As he regarded her, leaning against the table, taking another slow mouthful of his brandy, then laying the glass down again on the table edge, Luisa frowned across at him in honest puzzlement. 'So, you really do think I'm a spy. How ludicrous!'

'Ludicrous, is it?' Roth seemed to consider this judgement. 'You may wish me to believe that, but I'm afraid I believe otherwise.'

He paused and allowed his eyes to travel over her, taking in the slightly baggy T-shirt and the white trousers, which, though a little long, were a remarkably good fit. And suddenly he smiled. 'Isn't it funny,' he observed, 'how men's clothing always looks so sexy on a woman?'

How about that for changing the subject? Luisa gritted her teeth at him. 'I can't say I've ever thought about it.'

'I suppose it's the cut of them that gives you that appealing air of vulnerability.'

'Yes, of course, that would appeal to you— female vulnerability.'

He simply smiled in the face of her cutting comment. 'I suppose it does. I'm certainly not averse to it.' Then he caught her eye and smiled some more. 'I suppose it brings out the protective side of me.'

Luisa had to laugh. That was genuinely funny. 'You mean the predatory side.' She tossed him a scathing look. 'I find it impossible to believe that you could have a protective side.'

'Is that so?'

'Yes, it is.' She wished he'd stop smiling. There was something about that smile of his that made it impossible for her to speak as sharply as she'd like.

But he continued to smile, undermining her further, as he told her, 'I have many sides you have yet to discover.' Idly, dark eyes watching her, he played with the cue in his hand, twirling it as though it were a baton. 'Many, many sides, my dear Luisa.'

'Really? How interesting. However I have no wish to discover any of them.' To her annoyance Luisa felt the colour rise in her cheeks.

'No? That's a pity.' He looked into her hot face. 'I might have enjoyed revealing some of my more secret sides to you.'

As he said it, he winked, a deliberately wicked wink. Luisa felt the blood rush inside her like a geyser.

Damn him and his arrogance! Her hand tightened round her sherry glass as Roth turned away to play one final shot, sinking the ball into the pocket with irritating accuracy. And damn me, too, she added irritatedly, for reacting like a ninny!

She pulled herself together and addressed his still-turned back. It was time the tenor of this conversation was taken in hand a little. It was getting far too cosy for comfort. Well, not cosy exactly, but a little too personal.

In the tone of voice she normally reserved for difficult interviewees—measured, unflappable, infinitely patient—she asked him, 'So, why do you think I'm a spy? And what am I supposed to be finding out?'

Roth responded like the impossibly difficult interviewee he was. He quite simply didn't bother to answer. Instead, he laid down his cue, gathered up the balls, and set them out in a neat triangle on the table. Then he glanced across at her. 'Do you fancy a frame? There are some cues there in the rack on the wall behind you.'

Luisa glared at him and shook her head. 'I don't know how to play.'

'That's no problem. It'll be my pleasure to teach you.'

'I'd rather you didn't. I'll just watch, if you don't mind.'

'Of course I mind. That wouldn't be any fun.' He'd come to stand before the rack of cues behind her. And now, in spite of her protests, he proceeded to select one. He turned round and handed it to her. 'How does this one feel?'

'I really don't think——'

'I reckon it's about the right weight.' He guided her towards the table. 'Try it and see.'

'Look, this is silly.' Luisa stared down at her cue, excruciatingly aware of the hand that still cupped her elbow. 'I probably won't even manage to hit the ball.'

'Don't underestimate yourself. And don't underestimate your teacher.' He picked up his own cue. 'I'll break,' he said.

As he stepped away from her, Luisa gasped with relief. That brief physical contact with him had felt like a siege.

Clutching her cue, she watched as he leaned over the table and proceeded to execute a clean, perfect break. Then he stood aside. 'Your turn now,' he told her. He pointed to one of the balls. 'Try and pot that one first.'

Luisa leaned over the table and focused on the ball, feeling the cue stiff and awkward in her hands. Then, clumsily, she poked it forward and watched in dismay as the ball rolled off to the wrong side, miles from the pocket.

She pulled a face. 'I told you I'd be useless.'

'You're holding the cue all wrong.' He was coming towards her, returning the failed ball to its original position. 'Look, hold it like this. Straighten your arm more. And relax this one. Try to lean into it.'

As he spoke, he'd come behind her and was adjusting her arms. Luisa could feel the heat of his chest against her shoulders and the hard muscular strength of his arms against her own. His breath was in her hair, prickling her scalp, and she could smell the musky smell of him, clean and powerful, tingling in her nostrils, entering her bloodstream, rushing through her, making her blood burn.

This was worse than a siege, this was a total physical take-over!

'That's better now. Have another go.'

All at once he had stepped away again. Luisa stood motionless for a moment, struggling to calm herself and focus on the ball.

'Go on. Shoot!'

She shot. Blindly. Obediently. To her astonishment the ball dropped straight into the pocket.

'You see, I told you you could do it. All you needed was a good teacher.' Roth grinned across at her. 'Congratulations!'

It was silly. Nothing in the world could have mattered less to her than dropping a silly billiard ball into a silly pocket, but all the same she smiled back at him, foolishly delighted. 'Beginner's luck,' she protested. 'It won't happen a second time.'

'Do you want to take a bet on that?' He winked across at her. 'You're forgetting, you have the best teacher in the business.'

'Do I?'

'Absolutely.'

'Such modesty is touching.'

'Yes, I know. It's one of my most endearing characteristics.'

'You mean you have others?'

'Several. I told you—there are many sides of me you have still to discover.'

As their eyes met and held, a touch of pink warmed Luisa's cheeks. He's flirting, she thought, bemused. And I'm flirting right back at him. What an extraordinary occurrence. How on earth did it happen?

'Try this ball next.' He was pointing at the green one. 'You won't drop it in one, but just try to get it near the pocket. You'll have a better chance if you take it from the other side of the table.'

'OK.' Suddenly, Luisa had an appetite for the game. She crossed to the other side and took up her stance, wielding the cue precisely as Roth had told her, and joked as she took aim, 'Stand by for another miracle!'

It didn't fall into the pocket, but it came satisfyingly close. She glanced up, pleased with herself. 'Not bad, eh?' she observed. 'I think I'm beginning to get the hang of this.'

The game proceeded with Luisa hitting her fair share of balls into pockets—though she could tell that Roth was making things easy for her. What a pity he's not as nice as this all the time, she found herself reflecting, as she watched him neatly dispose of the yellow. Like this he's actually a lot of fun to be with.

But it was the very next moment that she made her wrong move.

Roth was about to take another shot—leaning across the table, drawing back his cue—when, acting automatically, Luisa darted forward and snatched up his brandy glass from the edge of the table.

Roth froze in mid-motion and tossed her a sharp glance over his shoulder. 'Playing mother again?' he growled. 'Please put the glass down.'

'But you were about to knock it over with your elbow!' Luisa felt her cheeks flush. Hadn't he told her before that he had an aversion to women who picked up after him? Women who, as he saw it, tried to organise him. But that hadn't been her intention. She'd acted without thinking.

'Put the glass down. I was not about to knock it over. I knew it was there. I knew its precise location.'

He probably had, Luisa recognised belatedly. He would have everything neatly stored in that computer brain of his. A little sheepishly she stepped forward and laid the glass down again.

'You can't resist it, can you? Interfering, I mean.' Roth straightened as he paused to chalk the end of his cue and threw her a look from beneath his lashes. 'Maybe that's why you don't have a boyfriend. That sort of thing's enough to drive a man crazy.'

'On the contrary, most men love it! Most men lap it up!' Luisa answered a little more vehemently than she'd meant to, for, surprisingly, his remark had hurt her a little. More calmly, she added, 'Most men like to be looked after.'

Roth had remained where he was, his dark eyes on her. 'It sounds to me as though you've been wasting yourself on the wrong men, the type who are really just looking for a mother.' He smiled a small smile and raised one dark eyebrow. 'That's not what men and women are supposed to be about.'

'And I suppose you know all about what men and women are about?' Her eyes flared as she looked at him with resentment and annoyance. And something else as well. Almost a kind of longing. She felt again the flicker of that wall of flames inside her.

Roth met her gaze. He smiled. 'I know enough.'

His eyes glinted as he said it, but it was a look that was amused and sensual and not really predatory in the least. He added, 'Perhaps I ought to give you a few pointers on the subject. It sounds to me as though you could use them.' And as he smiled, Luisa blushed. That had sounded almost protective.

She stared at the green baize and reflected that he was right. Anthony, for example, had been looking for a mother. Someone to look after him and give him advice. In the end, Luisa had grown rather dissatisfied with that role.

But she did not admit that to Roth Elman. Instead, she said, defensively, 'I don't think there's anything wrong with caring.'

'Nothing in the slightest. If it's genuine caring. Automatically picking up after someone isn't quite the same thing. I would call that an unfortunate compulsion.'

Luisa glared at him. 'I'm not compulsive. I don't pick up automatically. I only do it as a gesture of caring!'

And it was true. Her behaviour came naturally, but it was not compulsive. It had come from being a late child, born when her now dead parents were in their late forties. Growing up, she'd looked after them as much as they'd looked after her. She'd never found it an imposition to perform small services for those she cared for.

It was only as Roth smiled at her that Luisa realised what she'd said. His eyes flashed amusedly. 'How nice to know you care.'

Luisa blushed to her hair roots. 'I didn't mean that!' And neither did her actions demonstrate any such thing!

Yet perhaps they were bound up, it suddenly occurred to her, with the mysterious urge that occasionally afflicted her to reach out physically and touch him—in spite of the fact that she disliked him to the core! It was this powerful magnetic quality of his. It drew her and did strange things to her.

It was drawing her now, as he continued to look at her, his eyes roaming over her face, making her scalp prickle, a gentle intensity in his eyes that almost unhinged her.

He said, 'In that case, since I'm the exception to your caring rule, you should have no trouble curbing your picking-up impulses.'

'None whatsoever.'

'Good. That's a relief.' As he smiled, it seemed he was about to turn back to the billiard table. But, instead, he paused, his expression subtly altering. Then he put to her in a flat tone, surprising her totally, 'Does the name Gold Ingot mean anything to you?'

Luisa frowned. 'Yes, of course. They're my publishers.'

'So, you don't deny it?'

'Why should I deny it?'

He gave a half-shrug. 'Because you have a tendency to deny everything.' Then he turned away abruptly. 'I think it's my shot again.'

A minute later, taking up position across the table from her, he shot his next ball straight into the pocket. Then he straightened to cast a glance at her across the green baize. 'I take it no further explanations are necessary? I take it you now understand why I'm having you watched?'

Luisa understood nothing. She was totally mystified. 'What have my publishers to do with you setting spies on me?' she asked.

Roth shook his head impatiently. 'I've told you I'm tired of games.' Then he put to her, eyes narrowed, 'You had a meeting with them at their New York office just a few days ago, before you flew down to Nassau...' The dark eyes fixed her. 'Am I right?'

'Yes, you're right. So what?' Luisa countered.

'So what? I'll tell you what. I know what the meeting was about.'

'It was about a book we're planning to put together.' In spite of the suddenly hostile way he was behaving and the uncomfortable way it was making her feel, Luisa could not quite suppress a pleased little smile. She could scarcely believe it.

She was going to publish a book. It was something she'd dreamed of all her life!

Roth had laid down his cue and was facing her across the table, arms spread, hands leaning against the table edge. His eyes glittered across at her. 'And what is this book to be about?'

'It's a compilation of some of my interviews. The pick of the best I've done over the years. My speciality is character pieces, particularly of famous people.'

'Yes, I'm aware of that. I had you checked out.' Roth threw this information like a missile across at her. As she blinked, he added, 'I also know, however, that the book you're planning is not as you've told me... Its subject is to be something else entirely.'

He smiled a grim smile that lifted the hackles on her neck. 'However, I award you full marks for ingenuity. That was a most astute, almost credible lie.'

'It wasn't a lie. Why should I lie to you?'

'Because lying might be safer than confessing the truth. And there was always the chance that I might believe you.'

Luisa laid down her own cue. The game was over, nothing surer. In a reasonable tone she insisted, concealing her growing anxiety, 'But I wasn't lying. What I told you is the truth. Why do you keep insisting that I'm lying?'

'I keep insisting because I *know* you're lying.'

'But I'm not. I've told you the truth about the book.' She frowned. 'What on earth do you think it's going to be about?'

By way of a response Roth released a harsh breath. Then, on silent panther steps, eyes like rapiers, he began to circle the table towards her.

'I'll tell you what it's going to be about,' he snarled.

Luisa felt herself stiffen. Panic fluttered in her throat. He looked as though he was about to devour her.

'So, tell me,' she said, as calmly as she could.

He had drawn level with her now. He was virtually standing on top of her. The black eyes blazed down at her in fury. Then there was a terrible silence that seemed to echo round the room before he answered in one explosive syllable, '*Me*!'

'*You*?' Luisa was astounded. '*You*?'

'Yes, me! I'm to be the subject of your book!'

'But you're crazy!'

'No, *you're* crazy, Luisa.' His eyes blazed like beacons. '*You're* crazy if you think I'm going to let you do it!'

'But I've no intention of writing a book about you! Why on earth would I want to do that?'

'For the money it would bring you.' His tone was contemptuous. 'Isn't that why people in your profession do anything? And the more scurrilous the product, the more money it brings. That's why you came here... Why I found you skulking round my yacht... poking into corners you had no business poking into... You were looking for some dirt to spice up your story!'

Luisa's jaw had dropped open. Surely he couldn't be serious? Surely this was just another of his random insults?

Well, even if it was, she didn't intend to let him off with it. She tilted her chin at him, offended and angry. 'I'm not that kind of writer. I don't go looking for dirt. What I write about people is fair and honest. If I was writing about you—which I'm not, I can promise you—I'd have approached you about it openly. That's the way I work.'

'You expect me to believe that? You must think me a fool. Remember, I caught you skulking around one of the private cabins on my yacht.'

'I was looking for Rita! We've already been through that!'

'Yes, and I didn't believe you then, and I don't believe you now.' He paused and took a deep breath. 'No, that isn't quite true. You almost convinced me. In spite of all the evidence, I thought I might be wrong, that the story you were spinning me might actually be the truth.

'That was why I offered you the chance to leave. I knew that you would go if your story was true—after all, Rita isn't here, so there'd be no point in your staying.' His eyes sliced through her. 'I also knew,' he continued, 'that if you were lying you *wouldn't* leave. If your real reason for coming here was the reason I suspected—namely to grub up some story for your unauthorised biography—then you'd find some way to stay...'

He paused and smiled a cold, damning smile at her. 'And, guess what? Surprise, surprise, you stayed!'

'I only stayed because I thought you could lead me to Rita! I didn't think I'd have much chance of finding her on my own.'

'Spare me more lies!' With a sudden violent fury, Roth snatched up one of the billiard balls and sent it hurtling across the green baize, sending the other balls spinning and ricocheting like an explosion.

Then he rounded on Luisa. 'You're as bad as she is! She's nothing but a spiteful, vengeful bitch. And it seems you're the same! What a pretty pair you make!'

Luisa was flabbergasted for a moment into silence. Then she said, as the obvious gradually dawned on her, 'You've dumped her, haven't you? The affair is over?'

He did not answer her, but there was really no need to. He'd scarcely be saying such things if the romance was still in progress.

Instead, he said, 'I suppose it's my own fault for letting on to her that there were several publishers after my story...' His eyes narrowed. 'Needless to say, including Gold Ingot.'

He continued between clenched teeth, 'Hell hath no fury... I know that's what they say, but I never suspected for one moment that she'd go to the lengths she's gone to to get her pound of flesh...'

As he paused, Luisa watched him, mentally completing the bitter saying. Hell hath no fury like a woman scorned. Now she knew for certain that Rita had been dumped.

But she didn't dwell on that. She listened in silence as he continued, 'I didn't actually believe her when she threatened to sell my story—or rather to sell the part about what a bastard I am.' He smiled a twisted smile. 'That was in spite of the fact that she told me she was already on the look-out for a biographer...'

Luisa could scarcely take in what he was saying to her. She blinked at him. 'Are you really talking about Rita?'

'Such innocence.' His eyes glittered at her like demons. A pulse of barely controlled fury beat against his cheekbone. 'So, you see, I know exactly why you're here... You're the biographer your sister threatened me with. You're here to try and dig up some dirt on me... After all, Rita's story about how I broke up her happy family then heartlessly rejected her isn't quite enough, is it? You need a little more meat than that to fill your book.'

Luisa had suddenly gone cold as she absorbed what he was saying. So, after all, he really had been deadly serious in his allegations that she was a spy.

She opened her mouth to protest. 'But you can't really think——?' But that was as far as she got. Roth was interrupting her.

'I don't think. I *know*. You and your sister are in this together. She out of revenge, you out of pure greed. As I said before, what a pretty pair you make!'

'But that's not true. I——'

But again he interrupted her. 'However, in spite of all your clever ploys, you won't succeed. There'll be no book. That I can promise you. Your charming sister is to be denied her pound of flesh, and you...' He paused a moment to catch her jaw in his long, strong fingers. 'And you, my pretty little muck-raker, will have no story to tell. Except perhaps the one about how I found you out.'

He released her abruptly, as though he feared contamination. 'In the meantime, until I decide what to do with you, I intend to keep you here.'

Then he was striding past her, like a whirlwind, making her hair fly up from her shoulders. He only paused for an instant to add menacingly over his shoulder, 'I'll make you regret the day you decided to mess with me!'

CHAPTER FIVE

'IF YOU don't mind, I want to make a phone call. To England.'

'An SOS? I wouldn't bother.'

It was the following day and, after breakfasting in her cabin, Luisa had gone up to the main sun deck in search of Roth. She'd found him having breakfast after his regular morning jogging session, still dressed in trainers, T-shirt and shorts.

'Join me,' he invited now, his manner friendly, as though none of last night's unpleasantness had ever happened.

Two-faced swine, Luisa thought to herself. Out loud she said, 'I've already had breakfast, thanks.'

'Then just join me for a coffee.' He motioned to the empty chair across the table. 'As long as you don't mind sharing a table with someone who's just done fifty laps of the main deck. Normally, I shower and change first, but this morning I was too hungry.'

He did not look like a man who'd just run fifty laps of anything. The dark hair was a little sleek with perspiration and he had the glow about him of physical exertion, but otherwise he looked as splendid and unruffled as ever. Fifty laps, to Roth Elman, was evidently a doddle.

That was both irritating, Luisa decided, and rather impressive.

But she did not accept his invitation. She had no desire for a repeat of last night's fireworks. Though he was smiling benignly enough at her now, she had learned how rapidly those gentle smiles of his could turn into thunderclaps of terrible anger.

She said, 'I've already had a pot of coffee. I just came to ask you if I could make a phone call.'

'To England, you said?'

'Yes. To my sister's house. I want to find out if there's any news. For all we know, she's already back there.'

'That would be good news. But I somehow doubt it.'

Luisa also doubted it. Even if the affair was over—which it must be if what Roth had told her was true—she somehow couldn't imagine her lovelorn sister just hopping on a plane and flying back to her husband. She was probably holed up somewhere, nursing her broken heart.

But Luisa had to find out for sure before she made her next move.

She stuffed her hands into the pockets of her shorts and frowned at Roth. 'So, do I have your permission? Can I phone England?'

'You have my permission.' He took a bite of waffle and washed it down with a mouthful of black coffee. 'I'll get one of the stewards to bring a phone to your cabin—unless you'd like to make the call from my stateroom?'

His stateroom. Unsummoned, across Luisa's brain flashed a Technicolor picture of a dimly lit room, all gold silk draperies and thick soft rugs, dominated by a vast inviting bed. She had to fight the flush that rose to her cheeks. She said, 'No, thank you. A phone in my cabin will be fine.'

She felt his gaze graze her face and she could sense his amusement as he repeated his offer. 'My stateroom would be more comfortable.'

'I've no doubt it would.' Luisa narrowed her eyes and glared at him. 'But, as I said, my cabin will be fine. I expect the phone call to be very brief.'

'I expect it will be, if you phone at this hour.' Roth glanced at his watch as he poured himself more coffee. 'You're aware that in England it's not even five o'clock?'

'Yes, I'm aware. I was going to wait an hour or so. Alan's an early riser. He'll be up by six.'

'Then I'll arrange for the phone to be brought to you in an hour or so.' He turned his attention back to his waffles.

'There's something else.' As Roth turned back to her curiously, Luisa elaborated, 'I want to call my hotel in Nassau. All my stuff's there and I'm still paying for my room. I'm afraid that's an extravagance I really can't afford. I want to cancel my room and ask them to store my things for me... Until I can manage to get back,' she added pointedly.

'And who knows when that will be?' He polished off another waffle, wiped his fingers on his napkin and tossed it down on the table. 'I fear we could be here for quite some time yet.'

'You mean here on board the yacht?' Her stomach clenched nervously. 'I hope you weren't really serious,' she added tightly, 'in that threat of yours last night to keep me here indefinitely. I suspect that would probably be illegal.'

Roth ignored that veiled threat of recourse to the law. He raised one jet-black eyebrow and tossed an unconcerned glance at her. 'What I actually meant was here in this part of the Caribbean—which, alas, is rather a long way from Nassau.

'But it might please you to know,' he added as she scowled at him, 'that we will actually be disembarking for a while this afternoon.'

'Where?' For no good reason, Luisa felt a spurt of optimism. At least on dry land she would be less at his mercy. In spite of the huge size of the yacht, trapped here on board with him, she felt distinctly claustrophobic.

'Where?' she said again. 'Where are we going?'

'Bird Island. A very pretty little place. We ought to be there in time for lunch.'

'Good.' Luisa started to take her leave of him, smiling to herself, feeling heartened by this new development. Any change in the current situation could only be positive. 'I'll expect the steward to bring the phone to my cabin in about an hour, then.'

Roth watched her go, chewing his waffle thoughtfully. Then he observed, just before she stepped out of earshot, 'Don't get too excited, will you? Our spies will be coming with us—keeping an eye on every move you make!'

Luisa sat in her cabin waiting for the phone to arrive and pondering her reaction to Roth's parting shot.

The truth was she was too confused to decide how she really felt about it. Did she really want to escape him and go back to Nassau? Or would it be better for her to stick with him? She just wasn't sure.

And the reason she was confused was very simple. She knew so little about what was really going on. Where was Rita? Was the affair really over? Was any of what Roth had told her last night actually true?

She focused on that last puzzle. If it was true, it would explain a lot. It would explain why Roth wished to keep an eye on her. In his position, to be honest, she would probably feel the same. Who wanted some grubby muck-raking biographer poking among one's private affairs, hoping to uncover some hidden scandal? Especially when, as in Roth's case, there was probably a great deal to discover!

She frowned. However, it was insulting in the extreme that he should have cast her in the role of muck-raking biographer! No less than he, she herself despised the breed. And Roth, if he was any judge of character, ought to be able to see that she did not belong in that category.

That thought brought her directly back to Rita and the threats Roth had told her Rita had made.

Could Rita really have behaved so despicably? she wondered. To be truthful, Luisa found it hard to believe. The elder sister she had always known was a warm-hearted person, not the spiteful virago Roth had painted her. It wasn't possible, surely, that Luisa had totally misjudged her sister?

And yet, she reminded herself, Rita had already surprised her once. Less than a week ago she would have insisted it was impossible that her sister might be capable of leaving her home and family and running off to have a torrid affair with some man. Yet that was precisely what had happened. So maybe the rest was true as well.

But she could not accept it. Roth must be lying. He must have invented that story in order to cover up the real reason why he wanted to keep her captive. It just wasn't possible that Rita could be so vindictive.

Her thoughts were interrupted by a knock on the cabin door. She rose to answer it and found the young steward standing there.

'With the compliments of Mr Elman.' He held out a mobile phone to her. 'If it's all right, I'll come back to collect it in half an hour.'

Luisa nodded. 'That's fine.'

She dialled England first. Alan answered almost instantly. 'Luisa!' he blurted anxiously as soon as he heard her voice. 'What's the news? Have you found Rita?'

Luisa felt her heart sink. 'No, I'm afraid not. I was rather hoping she might be back with you.'

She heard Alan sigh. 'No such luck. On the contrary, she seems to be planning on staying.' He went on, 'She phoned last night, asking after the children, saying that she'd left Nassau but was still in the Bahamas.' He sighed again. 'But she refused to tell me where.'

This was not good news. Luisa felt her heart sink further. All the same, she assured Alan, 'Don't worry. Somehow I'll find her.'

Easier said than done, she reflected defeatedly, as a few minutes later she completed her call to

Nassau. Rita might have been on the moon for all the progress she was making finding her!

As she reflected glumly on this gloomy state of affairs, there was another knock on the cabin door—the steward had come back for the phone.

Luisa rose to her feet. 'Here you are,' she told the steward, pulling the door open and holding the phone out to him. But as he reached out to take it from her, Luisa froze in her tracks. Suddenly she couldn't take her eyes off what he was holding in his other hand.

She could hardly speak. Her heart was leaping with excitement. 'I see you've got some mail there,' she finally managed to blurt out, just as the steward was about to move away.

The young man nodded. 'It's just arrived. It's mostly for Mr Elman. I'm on my way to deliver it to him now.'

As he spoke, he held up the wad of letters in his hand and Luisa's heart almost burst right out of her chest as she could see now, even more clearly than before, the topmost letter and the neat scrawl it bore—a hand she had been familiar with all her life.

She swallowed. This letter had been sent by Rita!

Her blood pounding, she bent towards the wad of letters. 'What a pretty stamp,' she observed, struggling to sound casual. Then with an innocent smile she reached out for the letter, as though to take a closer look at the stamp, and peered as hard as she could at the postmark.

But she couldn't make it out. It was a hopeless muddy blur.

Then, with trembling hands, she turned the letter over and very nearly let out a cry of triumph—for there, printed in blue across the back, was the name and address of a hotel. Beachside Hotel, Azura, it said.

She handed back the letter, grinning broadly. Now she knew where Rita was staying—or at least where she'd been staying until very recently!

As soon as the steward had departed, Luisa flew excitedly indoors to consult the map on her cabin wall. And in an instant she had found it, the island of Azura, only a stone's throw from Bird Island, where they were heading!

She let out a cheer of triumph. It couldn't be a coincidence that Roth was headed for Bird Island. It must mean that Rita was still on Azura and that something very definitely was in the air. Possibly a reconciliation—if there had ever been a breakup.

She smiled a determined smile. Whatever was going on, she intended to make sure that she was a part of it—that she had a chance to speak to Rita before she ruined her life totally.

And Roth needn't worry about keeping an eye on her. For, from now on, she'd be sticking to him like glue!

As she contemplated this thought with oddly mixed feelings, the yacht dropped anchor off the coast of Bird Island.

'Did you make your phone calls? Is everything in order?'

They were standing on the fore deck, waiting to leave the yacht, watching as the speedboat that had been sent to collect them approached in a wide arc from the little jetty, wings of creamy foam spraying out from its bows.

Beyond, Bird Island glittered in the sun, like a jewel of a thousand different shades of green.

'Yes, thanks.' Luisa turned to look at Roth. 'My hotel in Nassau has cancelled my room and they've agreed to look after my stuff until I can pick it up.'

'And your phone call to England. Was that a success?'

What a fraud he was! Not a flicker had crossed his face, though he knew perfectly well that her call to Alan had drawn blank. Though what he didn't know, Luisa reflected with a fraudulent smile of her own, was that not only did she now know where her sister was, but she knew also that he knew and that a meeting was on the cards!

She doused her inner smile and assumed an air of resignation. 'I'm afraid there's no word of Rita returning to England. You were right about that. She's still somewhere out here.'

'Of course she is.' He tossed her a sharp glance. 'But then you already knew that, didn't you?'

Luisa was thrown for a moment. Then she remembered. He had accused her last night of being in criminal partnership with Rita. It was an invention, of course. How could it be otherwise when the whole story of Rita's supposed threats was a lie from start to finish?

But again she wondered: What was going on? Why this elaborate screen of deception? What was the truth that he was so determined to keep it from her?

Well, she would soon find out. The speedboat had come alongside now, and Roth was leading the way off the yacht. All she had to do was make sure she didn't let him out of her sight!

As it turned out that proved to be no problem. A limousine was waiting for them by the jetty. Roth opened the rear door and invited her to climb in.

'We're going shopping,' he informed her, climbing in alongside her and instructing the driver to head for the town centre.

Luisa was peering out the window at the sights and sounds of the little harbour, only half listening to what he was saying. 'Shopping?' she asked without curiosity. 'What kind of shopping?'

'Clothes shopping, my dear.' He cast a dark eye over her, observing the slightly rumpled white trousers and T-shirt. 'We can't have you going around in drag indefinitely. Just for a change, I'd quite enjoy seeing you in a dress.'

Luisa snapped round then to look at him. 'You can't buy clothes for me! I don't have any money,' she told him.

'Then it's just as well I do, or our trip would have been wasted.' He smiled an amused smile. 'We're going to get you some new outfits.'

'But I don't need any new outfits! I'm fine as I am.'

'You're not bad, I confess. As I told you last night, you look quite sexy done up in men's clothes.'

He let his eyes drift over her, a look of mischief on his face, causing Luisa's skin to prickle and grow warm. Then, as she fought to hold his gaze, he added, winking, 'But I'm afraid you can't hold on to these trousers forever. The young deck-hand who lent you them needs them back.'

Luisa hadn't thought of that. 'I see,' she responded. 'In that case, I suppose I'd better get something.' Then she narrowed her eyes at him. 'But nothing too expensive. As soon as I can, I intend to pay you back.'

'That won't be necessary.'

'Oh, but I insist!'

'Let's not fall out about it.' He leaned across her suddenly, making her jump back defensively in her seat. 'We're here,' he said, pushing the door open. 'Let's go and see what we can find.'

They had stopped, to Luisa's horror, in front of the kind of high-class shop she had never set foot in in her life before. She would never have dared! She would scarcely have dared look in the window!

As Roth proceeded to steer her towards the entrance, she dug in her heels. 'I'm not going in there!'

'Why ever not? They have some lovely stuff.'

'Yes, I can well imagine.' From beneath the plate-glass doorway seemed to drift the heady scent of expensive silk and leather. Luisa glared at Roth mutinously. 'This isn't my sort of shop! I couldn't afford a set of buttons from this place!'

But Roth continued to steer her. 'OK, we'll buy the stuff for me. You can simply wear it for a while, then chuck it away.' So saying, he whisked her over the threshold. 'Is that OK?'

Luisa glared at him tightly. It wasn't OK, but already they were being approached by a smiling assistant, as expensive-looking and highly polished as her wares, and Luisa was suddenly reluctant to make a scene.

She scowled at Roth. 'OK,' she muttered. 'But, remember, I'm not keeping a single thread of it!'

Roth simply smiled and turned to the assistant. 'I'd like you to help this young lady to choose some new outfits. Skirts, shoes, dresses, the lot.' He cast an amused glance at Luisa. 'She wants to change her image.'

Pig! Luisa smothered an answering smile of amusement. She wasn't just changing her image, she was going from the ridiculous to the sublime!

Oblivious of their private joke, the elegant assistant scanned Luisa. 'I'm sure we have plenty of things to suit you.' Then she dazzled her with a smile. 'Please come this way.'

To begin with Luisa was totally out of her depth. As the assistant—and Roth, for he had plenty to say!—began riffling through the rails of blouses and skirts and dresses, holding up garments for her opinion, she simply stared at them dumbstruck, muttering things like, 'How beautiful!' and, 'That's exquisite!'

She had never even dreamed of trying on such garments, let alone faced the prospect of walking out of a shop with them!

But, gradually, when it became clear that she was not to be allowed out of the shop until she had chosen a new, if temporary, wardrobe, Luisa began to enter into the spirit of the thing. She had no choice, so she might as well enjoy it. And enjoying it, she soon discovered, proved remarkably easy!

'I'll try on the blue dress,' she told the assistant, 'and that blouse and that skirt and those red silk trousers.'

'Then you'll need the red top as well.' Roth added it to her pile. 'And I think you should try this white dress as well.'

The man was crazy, Luisa decided, as the assistant led her to the changing-room and she took the opportunity to hiss at him, 'When I go back to Nassau you can auction it all off for charity!' These clothes were far too good just to throw away!

Roth simply smiled and winked at her. 'Good idea,' he agreed. 'Now go and try it all on. I want to see what you look like.'

What she looked like, without a doubt, was a million dollars. Fascinated, Luisa stared at her reflection as she emerged from the changing-room for the third time, wearing yet another stupendous outfit, and came to stand before Roth and the huge wall mirror. She didn't blame him for applauding and whistling beneath his breath. These magnificent clothes would have made anyone look great!

'We'll take the lot. Now show us some shoes and handbags.'

Luisa blinked at him. 'You're crazy! I don't need all this stuff!'

'Don't argue. Just consider it all the more for the auction.' Dismissing her protests, Roth turned away and pointed. 'How about those sandals over there?'

Luisa was feeling slightly shell-shocked by the time they left the shop, Roth having instructed the assistant to deliver all the packages to the yacht.

When he took her arm, she did not bother to protest and neither did she particularly feel the gesture was out of place. She probably looked as dizzy and shell-shocked as she felt. He probably thought she was in need of a little support!

'Lunch?' He was glancing down at her as they made their way along the street. 'I know a terrific little restaurant just round the corner.'

Luisa nodded. 'Just as long as we don't have to do any more shopping! I don't think I could survive any more of that.'

He laughed. 'You didn't do badly for a beginner. I could see there was a definite untapped talent lurking there.'

'Destined to remain untapped!' Luisa made a face at him. 'What happened back there was strictly a one-off!'

'But you enjoyed it, didn't you?' He squeezed her arm and looked at her. 'You didn't really find it such an awful chore?'

'Does a child enjoy Christmas?'

Her tone was jokey, but all the same as her gaze collided with his she was aware of a strange tightening deep inside her. She *had* enjoyed it. She had enjoyed it immensely. And not just because of all the extravagant acquisitions—which, after all, weren't really hers, they were simply on loan to her. She had enjoyed it most of all because of Roth.

He'd been so relaxed, so attentive, so downright *nice* with her! He'd made the whole thing fun. He'd been warm. He'd been interested. It was he, not the clothes, who'd made her feel like a million dollars!

They'd turned the corner and now the restaurant was in sight.

'I hope you're hungry?' Roth demanded, glancing down at her. His dark eyes twinkled. 'Personally, I'm starving. Spending money always gives me an appetite.'

Luisa smiled, but deep inside she was filled with a new anxiety. Why was he being so nice to her? What was he up to?

And, more importantly, more frighteningly, what was happening to her? Why did she suddenly feel as though she were floating six feet off the ground?

'Dress for dinner.'

Those had been his last words to her as, finally aboard the yacht again, they had parted company. As she nodded awkwardly, he'd winked. 'I leave the choice to you.'

Luisa had chosen the blue dress with the slim, shaped skirt and the wide scooped neck that showed off her suntan. She stood in it now, matching blue sandals on her feet, matching blue purse on the bunk bed behind her, gazing at her reflection as though at a stranger.

They had spent two hours over lunch this afternoon, consuming a bottle of wine and three delicious courses, and chatting amiably about nothing in particular. Not a single bitter word had passed between them.

Afterwards, they'd gone for a stroll through the little town, in and out of back-streets, ending up along the sea front. And again, there had been not a moment of disharmony. Every moment, in fact, had felt like tremendous fun.

It had been after five when they'd climbed on board the yacht again and each gone their own way to their separate quarters. And it wasn't until then that it had suddenly struck Luisa that what was happening couldn't be real.

She'd walked into the cabin and seen the pile of packages, whose luxurious scent had seemed to fill the air around her, and had suddenly wondered if it was all a dream.

Feeling dazed, one by one, she'd up-ended the packages and spilled their incredible contents over the bunk bed. What was she doing with all this stuff, even on loan? Girls like her didn't wear such clothes.

Then she'd stared into space. More to the point, girls like her didn't become all dreamy and unhinged by a few pleasant hours spent in the company of a man like Roth!

Dressed in her new swimsuit, she'd gone for a swim in the pool, hoping a bit of strenuous exercise might help to clear her head. Then she'd sat out on the sun deck, grateful there was no sign of Roth, and watched the sun go down over the horizon. It was after half-past seven when she had returned to her cabin, her head still no less befuddled than before, and suddenly uneasy at the thought of joining Roth for dinner.

Under the shower she'd toyed briefly with the idea of rebellion. He had asked her to dress, meaning in one of her new outfits. But what if she were to wear her borrowed white trousers and T-shirt? Would such a gesture make her feel any better? Less confused? More in control?

But she rejected the idea. She would simply look foolish. It would be the equivalent of a public announcement that she couldn't handle the situation.

And what, after all, was there to handle anyway? He'd taken her to lunch, been nice to her for once, and bought her a couple of expensive frocks, because, for some obscure reason, it had amused him to do so, and that was really the long and the short of it. There was nothing to be handled. Nothing at all.

And so she had slipped on the new blue dress, her heart catching at the sensuous feel of it, and had strapped her feet into her new blue sandals, then squirted some of her new scent over her neck and shoulders and turned towards the mirror to examine the result.

At first, in this strange mood of hers, it had felt like looking at a stranger. But she had breathed deeply and scowled at herself and told herself not to be silly. This was no stranger. This was the same old Luisa. The only difference was she was wearing a two-thousand-dollar frock! Beneath that silken sapphire exterior nothing had altered.

Particularly not my head, she told herself firmly, without elaborating precisely what she meant by that. Inside my head nothing has altered.

She picked up the blue purse and glanced at her watch. Almost eight-thirty. It was time she was on her way.

Outside on the gangway, she glanced up at the stars, which looked so close that it was as though they were falling towards her.

Then on brisk, determined steps, in her new blue sandals, she headed for the stairway that led up to the upper deck, to the dining-room, where Roth was waiting.

CHAPTER SIX

'SPECTACULAR! That's how you look—quite spectacular!'

Luisa smiled and accepted the flute of champagne Roth held out to her. If they were trading compliments, she could easily have said the same to him. In the immaculate black silk suit he was wearing, the slim dark tie and perfect white shirt, he was looking nothing if not spectacular. In fact, spectacular, she decided, was an understatement. He looked like some god who had dropped down from heaven.

But she kept that to herself and levelled a look at him. 'So you reckon I don't look too bad for a grubby, muck-raking journalist?'

Two straight black eyebrows lifted, but only for a moment. He met her level gaze without a flicker. 'I see you've recovered fully from the rigours of our little shopping spree.'

'I'm glad to say I have.' She took a mouthful of champagne. It danced delightfully against her palate, in much the same manner as her spirits were suddenly dancing. Yes, she had made a full recovery.

It had happened on the short journey from her cabin to the dining-room and it had been triggered, she felt certain, by that quick glance at the stars.

For in that moment, as she had looked up at them and they had seemed to pour down on her, it had suddenly crossed her mind that somewhere not so far away her very own sister might be gazing at the same stars. Gazing at them and dreaming of the man she adored—and whom Luisa was on her way to join for dinner!

She had felt ashamed of herself then, and of her earlier confusion. Sharply, she had reminded herself why she was here. Not to become fuddle-headed about Roth Elman, but to stop her sister from throwing away her life on him! Instantly, everything had come once more sharply into focus.

And now, perfectly at ease with herself and her surroundings, she drank more champagne and glanced round at the dining-room.

'What a beautiful room. It's quite extraordinary. Not the sort of room one would expect to find on board a yacht.'

'Isn't it? And what would one expect to find on board a yacht?' He was leaning lightly against the mahogany sideboard, watching her with an amused glint in his eye. He knew, of course, that she'd never been on board a yacht like this before.

'I really don't know.' Luisa shrugged and shook her head. 'Perhaps I might have expected something a little more... *basic*.'

She smiled as she said it. The last thing this place was was basic! With its crystal chandelier, polished hardwood table, expanse of thick, soft carpet, gleaming silver and sparkling crystal it was more like something out of some English stately home!

She glanced at him and added with just a hint of criticism, 'If this is what your yacht's like, I wonder how you live at home?'

'Which home in particular?' His tone was slightly cutting. And she deserved that, Luisa reflected. It was really none of her business to pass scathing judgement on his standard of living!

Yet that slight edge to his tone had rather pleased her. She relaxed even more. Things were definitely back to normal!

She met his gaze, unabashed. 'How many homes do you have?'

'Four at the last count.' The dark eyes held hers. He reached into the ice bucket at his elbow. 'More champagne?' he enquired, lifting out the bottle.

Luisa held out her glass. 'Four houses. Good heavens! You can't get much chance to live in any of them.'

'They all get their share of me.' He splashed champagne into her glass, then into his own, returned the bottle to the ice bucket and leaned more comfortably against the sideboard. 'I do my best not to make any of them feel left out.'

So, he was in one of his glib, unfazable moods. It was a mood she knew well. It was his media mood. The mood he seemed able to switch on at will whenever he was faced with members of the Press. Luisa wondered if it was her reference to her own professional status that had caused him to assume this familiar mantle.

But whatever had triggered it, it suited her perfectly. She felt right at home being treated as a journalist. And behaving like one. She proceeded to do so.

'So, where are all these homes of yours?' Her tone was politely enquiring. It was a tone that interviewees, as a rule, responded well to, though she recognised with an inner smile that it would only irritate Roth.

She knew also that he would disguise his irritation.

He did. He smiled back at her. 'They're scattered about the globe, in various places where it is convenient for me to have a home.'

'Aren't you going to tell me where?'

'Why, are you planning on visiting? Don't worry, if I decide to invite you, I'll send you very precise directions.'

He gave nothing away and he did it with such charm that, while driving his interviewer mad, he delighted his audiences. You had to hand it to him, he was a pro.

'That'll be the day, when you invite a journalist to your home!' Luisa stepped out of her professional role to make a personal observation. 'I shouldn't think any journalist has ever stepped over your threshold.'

'Not to my knowledge. Until now, that is, of course.' He raised his champagne flute in a mock-salute. 'I congratulate you on being the first.'

But it was not an accolade she had any right to—not that he had intended to flatter her! Luisa narrowed her eyes at him and said in a more serious tone, 'I didn't come here as a journalist. I've already told you that. I simply came here looking for my sister.' She smiled. 'I was strictly off duty at the time.'

Roth regarded her for a moment, then he raised black eyebrows. 'Even if I believed that, it would make no difference. Journalists are never off duty. Even when they're sleeping, I imagine, they're looking for a story. So, feel free to accept the honour. You were the first.'

A steward appeared at that moment and announced that dinner was ready. Roth waved Luisa in the direction of the table. 'Let's continue our conversation at the table.'

It was a long oval table, draped in a fine linen cloth and set all around with crimson velvet chairs. Roth seated himself at the head with Luisa on his right. She had never sat at so grand a table before.

But that was not what was on her mind now as the waiter brought soup in a highly polished silver tureen. She was watching Roth, taking in the sculpted dark profile, so self-possessed, so implacably set against her, and wishing, in spite of her own safe detachment, that he could accept the truth of what she'd just told him. It shouldn't matter, of course, but somehow it did that he had such a dreadfully low opinion of her.

Professional pride, she told herself. That's all it is.

She lifted her silver spoon and addressed the dark profile. 'Why do you hate journalists—all media people—so much?'

'Who said I hate them? Hate's a strong word.'

He had turned to glance at her, causing her heart to shift strangely. She could not quite make out the look in his eyes.

She dropped her own eyes to her soup and spooned up a mouthful. 'You act as though you hate them. What comes across *is* pretty strong. I can't believe you're not aware of that.'

'Are you talking about my behaviour in relation to you?' Again he turned to glance at her, and again Luisa experienced that strange sudden shifting in her breast. 'You and I,' he elaborated, 'are surely a somewhat unique case?'

Luisa swallowed her soup, not tasting a thing. 'No, I wasn't referring to that...to us,' she replied awkwardly. 'I was speaking generally. I really think you hate the media.'

'As I said before, hate's rather a strong word.' Roth swallowed some of his own soup before carrying on, 'There are some of them I despise, quite a few I have no time for...but, believe it or not, there are also some I admire.'

Luisa laughed. 'Now it's my turn to be disbelieving! Who do you admire? Go on, name names!'

'I wouldn't be so rash.' He turned to smile at her. 'Even those I admire I prefer to keep at a distance. I have no wish to encourage them to take advantage of my sympathies.'

'Then why do you have anything to do with any of them in the first place?' This was something she'd often thought, in fury, in private, as she'd watched some poor interviewer being literally torn to shreds by him. 'If, as you say, you'd rather keep your distance, why do you agree to be interviewed in the first place?'

'Sometimes I'm pressed into it.'

'You mean they drag you in chains?'

'Not exactly, no.' He smiled as he answered her. 'No one has ever subjected me to quite such drastic measures.'

'No, I'll bet they haven't. I'll bet no one would dare to!' She wished she hadn't said that. It sounded rather like a compliment. She carried on in less approving vein, 'The reason you appear on TV and give interviews to the papers, I imagine, is because you enjoy the publicity. You like seeing your face plastered over people's TV screens. You enjoy seeing your opinions given prominence in the newspapers!'

He was watching her, silver soup spoon poised in one hand, an odd echo, it occurred to Luisa, of the way she herself was sitting. He even seemed to be leaning forward at precisely the same angle.

'So, you think I'm entirely motivated by vanity, do you? I suppose you're not the only one, but I think you're mistaken.'

'Am I?' Her tone was scathing, though it occurred to her he might be right. He had a lot to be vain about, but she had never really thought he was. Arrogant. Opinionated. Ruthlessly clever. These were the characteristics she'd long found irritating in the extreme.

She spooned up more soup at the same moment he did and amended her earlier indictment slightly. 'I think what I really meant is that you must *want* the platform the media offers you. No one forces you, as you've admitted. You could always say no.'

'And frequently I do.'

'You also frequently say yes.'

'When I feel obliged to do so.'

'Obliged in what way?' She smiled a mocking smile. 'Don't try to tell me you do it out of a sense of public duty!'

'No, that sounds a little lofty.'

'I'm glad you agree!'

As their eyes sparked at one another across the table, in perfect unison they raised their soup spoons and drank.

Luisa laid down her spoon irritably. What the devil was going on? According to their body language, she and Roth were in perfect harmony—and they were supposed to be in the middle of a fight!

She laid her hands in her lap and regarded him stiffly. 'So, why do you do it? Tell me that!'

'I told you, I feel obliged.' He turned to face her. 'There are certain areas of business in which I'm considered an expert, and I do have quite a lot of valuable experience. When I'm asked to, if I consider it valid to do so, I have no objections to appearing in public and throwing light on certain matters that are on the public mind. My aim is to inform. No more than that. I think the general public has a right to be informed.'

Luisa couldn't argue with that! That was the basic premise of her job! It was because she believed that that she had become a journalist in the first place!

But she did not want to agree with him. As he sat facing her, she turned away, annoyed to discover that he had swivelled round, too.

She said, 'That's what the media is there for, to inform. Forgive me for saying so, but, if your aim is the same, how come you're always so hostile to interviewers and journalists? You seem to enjoy making their job as difficult as possible.'

'Do I?'

'I would say you do.'

'And why would you say that?'

As he leaned back in his chair, Luisa remained rigidly upright. She had a soothing sense of false harmony broken. In a more relaxed tone, she responded, 'You cut them to pieces. If they say the wrong thing, ask the wrong question, you're immediately down on them like a ton of bricks.'

As she spoke, she was thinking of one particular instance—a TV interview conducted by a colleague of hers that by the end had seen the poor guy virtually demolished. One could almost see his wounds and hear the dripping of blood.

She remembered watching the entire blood-bath in mingled horror and anger. The poor guy had only been doing his job, and Roth, in front of millions, had reduced him to life-support-machine fodder!

Roth had finished his soup and was laying down his spoon. 'I only do that when they deserve it.'

'Deserve it?' She was astounded. Her eyes rounded as she blinked back at him. 'How can anyone deserve the sort of maulings that you hand out?'

'They're free to maul back if they wish. And, indeed, some of them try.'

'To little effect. They're up against an expert!'

'Then they ought to make an effort to be experts, too. I only maul people—to use your terminology—who don't know what the hell they're talking about, who obscure the issue by asking stupid questions.'

What an arrogant attitude! Luisa gasped with disapproval. 'I might have known you'd come out with something like that!'

'It happens to be true. Think about it,' he invited, as the steward reappeared to clear away their soup plates and set before them a dish of steaming swordfish. 'I think you'll discover I'm perfectly justified in coming out with it.'

Luisa thought about it as the salad was brought and a bottle of white burgundy duly decorked and poured. Well, maybe, on reflection, she acknowledged reluctantly, that colleague of hers had asked a couple of dumb questions. She remembered wincing at one or two of them, knowing what would happen, anticipating with a shudder the lethal gleam of impatience they'd immediately ignited in Roth's eye.

But that was still no excuse for the way he devoured his victims and spat them out in tiny pieces into the watching public's living-rooms!

She helped herself to salad and trickled salad dressing over it. 'Just because someone occasionally asks a silly question that's no excuse for a public execution.'

'Now I'm an executioner?' He smiled, finding that amusing. 'So, why do they just sit there and let me execute them? They're supposed to be in charge. Why don't they execute me?'

As he spoke, he reached out for the silver bowl of salad dressing. As Luisa followed the movement, quite unaware of what she was doing, she reached out and obligingly pushed it towards him. 'You're too clever for them,' she said.

Suddenly both pairs of eyes were on the silver bowl—and on their two hands, one on either side of it. Then their eyes rose up to meet. 'Thank you,' Roth said.

Thank you for what? Luisa instantly snatched her hand away, as though she had been scorched, and dropped her eyes to the tablecloth. Was he thanking her for her gesture with the bowl of salad dressing or was he thanking her for the compliment she'd just paid him?

If the former, he had changed his attitude slightly! Previously, such a gesture would have been scorned. Previously, he would have been irritated by such a gesture.

Luisa found herself thinking she preferred his previous attitude. Her silly gesture, and his acceptance of it, had somehow felt disturbingly intimate.

That was why she said now, to banish the feeling, pretending that he had simply been thanking her for her compliment, 'I really wouldn't bother to thank me, if I were you. I didn't mean clever in a complimentary way.'

'No, of course you didn't.' But he was smiling, all the same, no doubt amused by her self-inflicted embarrassment. He poured a liberal measure of dressing over his salad. Then he glanced at her again. 'I wonder,' he put to her, 'how you would fare if you were to interview me?'

'That's something we'll never know.' And, frankly, she did not regret it. For suddenly Luisa was aware that her earlier sense of confusion, which she had thought she had overcome and put to flight forever, was there at her elbow, waiting to invade her again.

She tried to push it aside, taking a mouthful of swordfish. 'I don't do interviews with people like you.'

'No, I suppose you don't...'

'I only do showbiz people. Actors... Film directors...' she elaborated unnecessarily.

'And yet...' He was breaking off a piece of his swordfish. 'It would appear that you were planning to diversify a little... Maybe still are planning to, for all I know.'

'Meaning?'

'Meaning the book.'

'You mean the book about you?' She looked at him. 'There is no book about you.'

'I suppose not. Not now that I've clipped your wings a little.'

'I can assure you there never was a book, Mr Elman. I really wish you'd take my word on that.'

'Roth.' He smiled. 'My dinner guests call me Roth.'

Luisa's cheeks flushed crimson. She found it hard to look at him. The truth was she'd been on the point of calling him Roth, but at the last moment had changed it to Mr Elman. At the last moment she'd been afraid—not, she realised, of his reaction, but of hearing the sound of his name on her lips. It would, she had decided, sound far too cosy.

And yet that was ridiculous, she argued to herself, as the meal proceeded and dessert followed the swordfish. Every day of her life she called men by their first names, and it felt perfectly natural, not cosy in the slightest! Why should it feel any different when the man in question was Roth Elman?

That was a question she could address to a thousand different puzzles, she decided as, finally, coffee was brought. It was disconcerting and incomprehensible, but everything about Roth, and the way she reacted to him, was not as it was with other men.

And what was more she found it impossible to imagine ever meeting another man who was anything like him, or who was ever likely to have this unsettling effect on her. She ought to feel thankful for that, but inexplicably she did not. She simply felt confused as to why she should think such thoughts at all!

'Shall we have brandy outside? Or, in your case, sherry.'

So, he'd noticed and remembered what she'd drunk last night in the billiard room. Luisa nodded. 'Yes, it would be nice to have it outside.' Was it really only last night since they'd crossed swords in the billiard room? It seemed like a thousand lifetimes ago.

Roth instructed the steward to bring their drinks outside—along with the decanters, in case they wanted to top up!—then he was holding the door open, inviting Luisa to step ahead of him out on to the moonlit upper deck.

Luisa sighed as she crossed to lean against the handrail and gazed out across the shimmering starlit sea. She smiled. 'How I love these warm balmy evenings. I envy you being able to spend time here.'

'I wish I could spend more.' He was standing beside her, holding out to her her glass of sherry. 'It's one of the best places I know to relax.'

Luisa took the glass. She felt the brush of his fingers. Something flared inside her. But she did not pull away.

She said, 'You must need to take a break fairly often. I imagine the pressure must get to you at times.'

'So, you see me as the frail type, in need of frequent rehabilitation?' He had leaned against the handrail. He was smiling down at her. 'That's the first time anyone has ever said that.'

'I wasn't saying that and you know it very well!' He was about as frail, she was thinking, as a cageful of tigers! 'But you do,' she enlarged, 'lead a fairly pressurised life. Certainly, that's the impression I get.'

'It can be stressful at times, just like all jobs.' He took a mouthful of his brandy as she sipped her sherry. Their eyes met across the tops of their glasses. 'But I'm lucky, I'm one of these people who seem to thrive on stress.'

'I know what you mean.' Luisa lowered her glass. 'A bit of stress can sometimes work wonders. I've produced some of my best work under the threat of an imminent deadline!'

She shook back her hair. 'But for you the pressure must be constant. All those companies you run... All those decisions you have to make...'

He smiled. 'All those media interviews I have to endure...'

'Yes, that most of all.' She pulled a face at his teasing. 'That really must be the final straw. Who can blame you for taking off to the Bahamas from time to time?'

There was a pause. The moonlit night seemed to throb all around them. It seemed to Luisa she could almost hear the sigh of eternity and the rustle of starlight falling towards them.

Then he reached out to flick a stray strand of hair from her shoulder. 'And you, Luisa,' he said. 'What do you do to relax?'

'Oh, this and that.'

He had not moved his hand away. It was still curled there, softly, against her shoulder, brushing against her hair, making her scalp shiver.

'What kind of this and that?' He smiled. 'Be more specific.'

'I play sports... A bit of tennis in the summer. Badminton in the winter. I read. I watch films.'

'I also like tennis.' His hand touched her ear. A shiver went through her and seemed to nail her to the deck. 'And there's a court here on board. We ought to have a game some time.'

Luisa nodded. What a good idea, she had wanted to say. But the words never got any further than her head.

For suddenly she was incapable of all physical movement—even the simple act of speaking was beyond her. Every inch of her felt galvanised by the improbable sensations that were suddenly rushing through her like a tornado.

It had started with her ear and the side of her neck. Her skin had felt hot. It had started to tingle. Then, before she could stop it, the feeling was spreading, tentacles of fire licking against her senses, scorching her, fusing her muscles into immobility.

And the strangest thing of all was that it felt quite delicious, this feeling of being locked inside one's body and powerless in the face of the sensations that poured through it. Luisa felt not the faintest desire to resist it.

'We can do without this.'

Roth had laid his glass aside, and now he was taking hers, sliding it from her boneless fingers and placing it to one side on the wide wooden handrail. 'I think you would be more comfortable with both hands free.'

Luisa had no time to wonder what he'd meant. He smiled down at her, took her two hands gently in his and, as though nothing could be more natural, placed them on his shoulders.

Then he slid his arms round her waist. 'There, that feels better.'

He was right, it did. Luisa stared at her hands for a moment. They looked so small, so fragile against the broad shoulders of his black jacket. Then, even as she watched, these small fragile objects, as though of their own volition, slid slowly round his neck.

Instantly, her fingers made contact with his hair, thick and soft, and with the warmth of his neck. The sudden intimacy startled her. Her eyes flew to his face. All at once her heart was thundering in her breast.

Black eyes met hers, pouring into her, and the arms around her waist began to tighten, drawing her against him, burning through her dress.

For an instant her brow puckered. Was this really happening? Her lips parted to ask the question. But she never asked it. For that was when he bent to kiss her.

Luisa gasped and fell against him, fingers tightening in his hair as a shock wave of pure sensuous pleasure tore through her. All at once, from head to toe, spontaneously, she was in flames. Even her blood felt like molten fire in her veins.

It was his lips that had caused this remarkable sensation. They kissed like no other lips before. They moved against hers, devouring her, consuming her, with the raw, naked passion of a wild beast untamed.

Untamed and untamable. Wild and wicked. Cruel and masterful. Ferocious. Delicious.

His hands caressed her back, moving unhurriedly, kneading her spine, turning it to jelly. She loved the feel of those strong, supple hands.

Shamelessly, she longed for them to explore every inch of her.

'Luisa! Luisa!'

Hungrily, he kissed her. He kissed her as though he could never have his fill of her. And one hand was in her hair now, tilting her face towards him, holding her there against him, making her his prisoner, as his mouth scorched her lips, her cheeks, her temple, tying her stomach in knots, sending the blood surging through her.

The hand against her back had slid a little lower, caressing the womanly swell of her buttocks, pressing her thighs more tautly against his. And she could feel his desire, hard as a boulder against her. Desire knifed through her loins, making her tremble.

'Oh, Roth!'

Almost impatiently, one hand slid from his shoulder, caressing the deep, hard muscles of his chest. Then she was prising open the buttons of his soft silk shirt and slipping her hand inside to feel the warm flesh beneath.

She felt him shiver at her touch. The response was instantaneous. And as he moaned she felt an echoing shiver inside herself. Suddenly they were two souls, two electrified bodies, needing, craving one another, desperately.

That was when his hand slid up to her zip. It glided open as easily as a gossamer whisper. And, as it parted down her back, her dress dropped down over one shoulder. Luisa shuddered as his hand slipped in around her waist.

It was unbearable, that sudden contact of naked flesh against flesh. It was like a bolt of electricity suddenly charging through her.

'You're not wearing a bra.'

Luisa shook her head. 'No.' And every muscle and nerve-end in her body tensed, waiting for, longing for what she knew he was about to do.

His lips pressed against hers with an almost exploratory softness, teasing, making the breath catch in her throat. And all the while his hand, pushing her dress aside gently, was moving round from her back, circling her waist unhurriedly, then, fingers spreading to possess her totally, moving up to cup her breast.

At first, he was barely touching her. Like his lips, his hand was gentle. But then his lips grew more firm, his kiss hungrier and deeper, causing her blood to jump in feverish anticipation, scarcely able to endure the agony of waiting till the same fire in his lips flowed out through his hand.

Then his hand tightened against her, making her cry out with pleasure, his fingers circling, moulding, tearing her senses to pieces, mercilessly grazing the hard, ripe nipple.

She was like a rag doll in his arms. Breathlessly, she fell against him. The storm within her was uncontainable. She felt close to weeping for the wanting that filled her.

'Come. Let's make ourselves a little more comfortable.'

Roth kissed her face and drew away a little. She could see a question in his eyes. With her own eyes she answered him.

Then he was leading her across the deck, one arm firmly round her waist, and she was following him, her blue dress falling round one shoulder, her legs barely supporting her, her heart in hopeless turmoil, to the stateroom with the big gold bed.

CHAPTER SEVEN

AND it really *was* gold, just as she had once imagined!

The huge king-size bed that stood against one wall was draped in magnificent dull gold silk, gold-embroidered cushions were propped against the headboard, and even the magnificent headboard was framed in gilded wood. Heavy gold curtains hung by the windows, roped and tasselled, cascading richly, and the carpet beneath her feet, as she kicked off her sandals, was thick and soft and in a delicate shade of gold.

But Luisa was barely aware of all that as she stepped into the stateroom. All her attention was devoured by the longing inside her and the man at her side who had awakened that longing. She was consumed by that longing. She was weak and dizzy with the power of it.

'Come.'

Roth was guiding her, his arm lightly circling her waist, across the vast expanse of soft carpet. And all the while he dropped kisses into her hair and on her face, making her scalp burn, sending shivers of excitement down her spine.

Luisa clung to him, returning kiss for smouldering kiss. The desire in her was so strong that she felt she might explode.

Then they were standing by the bed. She could feel the silk coverlet against her legs. And Roth was reaching behind her, tugging the zip gently, so that at last it was released fully and her dress slid further down her shoulders.

Then he was taking her arms and laying them momentarily by her sides. The dress fell with a soft swish to the floor.

And now she was standing, raw and exposed, before him, only the whisper of white lace that was her panties ineffectually hiding her total nakedness.

A thrill went through her as he reached out to cup her breasts and she glanced down to see the smooth dark skin of his fingers against the delicate creamy white of her own flesh. Involuntarily, she pressed against him, feeling a quick dart of pleasure as, with his thumbs, he grazed the sensitive blood-gorged peaks.

'Now, what about me? Aren't you going to undress me?'

As he spoke, he had already shrugged off his jacket and was tossing it on to a gold-upholstered chair in one corner. Then he was tugging at his tie and unfastening the belt at his waist.

He bent to kiss her face. 'Why don't you help me?'

Perhaps she ought to feel shy. The thought passed through her head. After all, she had never been with a man like this before. But her hands went quite naturally to the buttons of his shirt, slipping open the remaining ones she hadn't undone earlier, impatiently tugging the shirt free from his trousers. Then, her open hands caressing the hard warmth of his shoulders, she was pulling the shirt away and letting it drop to the floor.

She'd seen him naked before, but not like this. In the warm golden glow of the lamps by the bed his body seemed harder, darker, more muscular, the hair-scattered skin somehow more luminous. With a sigh she bent to kiss the broad, powerful chest.

He caressed her hair, his fingers sliding against her scalp. Then, gently, he was drawing her face up to his again, pulling her against him, kissing her with raw passion. Luisa could feel the hectic unchained beat of his heart.

Then, still kissing her, one hand still twisting in her hair, with his other hand he was pulling at the buttons and zip of his trousers, freeing himself, pressing against her.

'How wonderful you are.' He was laying her on the bed, discarding her lace briefs, then lying naked beside her. 'And I knew it. I knew you would be wonderful like this.'

'I knew it, too.' Luisa's hands were in his hair, tugging, caressing, as he bent over her, kissing her. 'I knew that we would be wonderful together.'

And it was inexplicable, but she had. She had known it without even thinking. They had been meant for this moment. It was what they'd both been born for.

'My wonderful Luisa...!'

He buried his face against her breasts, his hands caressing her, moving like fire against her, while her hands, trembling a little, moved hungrily over him. Every inch of him enthralled her. Every inch of him was exquisite.

Then suddenly the lips that had been laying kisses along her breastbone shifted without warning to take hold of one hard nipple. A jolt went through her. Her back arched against him.

'Oh, yes!' she murmured. 'Oh, yes, Roth—please!'

But Roth was in need of no invitation. One hand caressing her flanks, the other cupping her aching breast, he drew the sensitive flesh deeper into his mouth. Tugging. Teasing. His tongue circling and strumming. Sending helpless pleasure through her. Making her cry out.

It was an awakening. She had never dreamed of ecstasy like this. The excitement that poured through her, twisting and tightening, was almost too excruciating to endure. It was like a tidal wave swallowing her, drawing her into its vortex. And, willingly, she surrendered. She longed to drown beneath its waves.

'Oh, Roth!'

As he raised his face once more to hers, his lips covering hers, bruising her with their passion, she sighed, her naked body pressing against him, shuddering, eager, offering its secrets.

If he did not take her now, she would die, she was thinking. Emotionally and physically she had reached the point of no return.

But that was when he surprised her. Drawing back a little, he gazed into her face with smouldering eyes.

'Perhaps we're going too fast. Perhaps we ought to slow down a bit.' He raised her hand and kissed it. 'Not that I want to. More than anything at this moment I want to make love to you.'

Luisa almost protested. She very nearly pleaded. Every fibre of her hungry, heated body was crying out silently, Take me! Take me!

But with an effort she remained silent. She would not shame herself by pleading. Though she was dying with desire for him, she must have a little pride.

'There will be time for all that.' He was caressing her face, that magnificent dark gaze of his burning down on her. 'But I want you to stay. I want you to spend the night with me.' He kissed her again. 'Will you, Luisa?'

Luisa looked back at him, feeling a strange happiness stir within her. Beyond the yearning in his face, beyond the carefully controlled passion, she could see warmth shining down on her. Warmth and affection.

She snuggled against him, pressing her lips against his neck. 'Of course I'll stay.' Her arms circled his neck. What she had just seen in his eyes was worth more, she suddenly realised, than the physical act of making love. What he had been offering her was a tiny, precious piece of his heart.

Roth was drawing her towards him now, almost protectively, kissing her brow, a faint smile on his lips. 'I don't imagine I'll manage to sleep a wink, of course... but I want you with me. I wouldn't sleep anyway without you. I couldn't bear for you to go.'

'Me, too.' Luisa kissed him. Her heart was singing. She wouldn't sleep either, she was perfectly sure of it. But she didn't care. It didn't matter. All that mattered was that he wanted her here with him.

But they did sleep, and soundly, arms wrapped around each other, like two innocent children, beneath the gold bedclothes.

Luisa was awakened by the sound of a helicopter.

She sat up with a start. Where was Roth? She was alone and abandoned in the big double bed.

The noise of the helicopter was growing louder, a rhythmic, clattering, ear-splitting sound. Luisa snatched the gold coverlet and wrapped it around her, then hurried to the window, pushing aside the curtains.

The great noisy beast was in the process of landing on the fore deck. And, standing in attentive readiness for its arrival, were Roth and several members of the crew. Who on earth could be on board? Luisa wondered curiously. Adjusting the coverlet, she peered through the window and waited.

At last, the wheels of the helicopter were making contact with the deck. The roar of the engine suddenly diminished. The whirling blades began to whirl more slowly. And then, out through the doorway, hair flying in the wind, stepped a tall, slim, stunningly elegant redhead. With a cry of delight, she rushed towards Roth. The next moment he had whisked her into his arms.

It struck Luisa, when she thought about it later, that in that moment, as she stood watching the little scene, she was assaulted by a wave of raw, burning jealousy, the like of which she had never experienced before. As she watched the embrace and the warm exchange of kisses, it tore at her insides and filled her mouth with bile. All at once, from top to toe, touched with ice, she was shivering.

With trembling hands, as the two figures moved out of sight, she dropped the curtain and stood very still. Her eyes could not focus. Her whole body had gone numb. It was as though someone had reached into her and torn out her insides.

Luisa crossed to the bed and sat down shakily. She stared at the wall, the gold-silk-covered wall, and through the agony that gripped her she could feel a new sensation stirring. Horror. Black horror. Had she taken leave of her senses?

And then it all came flooding in on her. The monstrousness. The lunacy. The disgrace and the utter shamefulness of what had happened last night.

What had she been thinking of, allowing such a thing to happen? How could she have done it? How on earth could she have behaved so badly?

How could she have romped stark naked on this bed with Roth Elman, allowing him intimacies she had allowed no man before? How could she have spent the night with him beneath these gold silk covers, her arms wrapped around him, her body clinging to his?

This was the man her sister was in love with. The man she had abandoned her family and was ruining her life for. And Luisa had betrayed her sister without even a thought.

Luisa rose stiffly from the bed and crossed to the chair where Roth had thoughtfully laid her things. She pulled on the lacy briefs and stepped into the blue dress. Until she had seen Roth embracing that other woman, she had literally forgotten all about Rita. It was unthinkable, it was disgraceful, but it was the truth.

She pulled up her zip and stepped into her blue sandals, glanced quickly in the gilt-framed mirror and pulled her fingers through her hair. Suddenly, she was desperate to be gone from this scene of betrayal. All she wanted was to escape, to be alone in her cabin.

The first thing Luisa saw as she stepped through her cabin door was the blue silk evening bag lying on her bunk bed. Roth must have retrieved it from the dining-room where she had left it and brought it here while she was still sleeping.

She closed the door behind her and stood staring at it for a moment. Why had he bothered? After all, it wasn't even hers. It was simply on loan to her, like everything else.

A shaft of pain pierced her. On loan. Like Roth. Then she closed her eyes, raised her face to the ceiling, and let the tears pour down her face.

Luisa was recovered by the time she emerged from her cabin, dressed in a pink linen skirt and matching pink blouse—one of the outfits Roth had splashed out on yesterday. She would have preferred to wear the old shorts and top he'd loaned her previously, but these, to her annoyance, had mysteriously disappeared.

She marched along the gangway, heading for the sun deck, noticing that the helicopter was still parked where it had landed.

He was there, as she had expected, finishing breakfast. A second place, she noticed with a fierce tightening inside her, had also been used recently, but for the moment he was alone.

She approached him with her head high, but as he turned suddenly to face her her step almost faltered and the breath caught in her throat. How could he smile at her that way? Did he have no shame for what had happened?

Evidently not. He continued to smile at her. 'Good morning,' he said. 'You're looking as lovely as ever.' Then a light touched his eyes. 'I won't ask if you slept well. I already know the answer to that.'

Fierce colour had touched her cheeks. Suddenly her blood was churning. Luisa threw him a cold glance. 'Who's the redhead?'

He did not answer immediately. The dark eyes had narrowed and the smile, all at once, had slipped from his face. Then he smiled again, mockingly. 'My sister,' he said.

'I'll bet!' Luisa glared at him. 'Does Rita know about your "sister"?' She spoke the word with a twist, making her disbelief plain. 'And does your "sister" know about Rita?'

'What's that to you?' He had turned away from her. Arrogantly, uncaringly, he was pouring himself more coffee. 'What right have you to pry into my private affairs?'

'I have every right. I'm Rita's sister. Or had you forgotten that small detail?'

'You mean like *you* did last night?' He turned to flick a scornful glance at her. 'These touching sisterly loyalties of yours would appear to come and go a little.'

Luisa flushed again and protested, 'I'm not proud of what happened. In fact, I'm deeply ashamed. It won't happen again.'

Roth nodded. 'No, I expect not. What a pity.' He threw her a lewd look. 'You're quite an explosive little bundle.'

'How dare you?' Luisa's fists clenched. She glared at him in anger.

But he simply smiled. 'Feel flattered. It was meant as a compliment.'

As he turned away again and took a mouthful of his coffee, Luisa glared at him in speechless anger. Yet through her anger she was aware of a deep sense of sadness, and a sense of regret that reached right down into her soul.

Last night who would have believed that things would sink to this level? Last night, as she'd looked into his face, she'd imagined she could see tenderness and caring. Even a tiny grain of affection.

But she'd been fooling herself. She'd seen no such thing. All she'd seen was the deceitful smile of a man who cared only for his own pleasures, who treated women like playthings.

She felt a gasp of pain, but quickly doused it. She'd had no right to him in the first place. It was her own fault that she'd been fooled.

Luisa swallowed and glared at him, summoning back the anger that had slipped away from her. In a tight voice she said, 'So where's the readhead now?'

'If you're so interested, go and look for her. That's your speciality, isn't it... searching through my yacht for missing women?'

'I'm not really interested where she is.' Luisa tossed her head defensively, hating herself for the way his indifference grazed against her.

It's on Rita's behalf that I care, she told herself. Rita's the one he's betraying, not me.

She started to turn away. She'd had enough of this conversation. She didn't even know what had possessed her to start it.

Then he stopped her in her tracks. 'You're going to be rid of me for a while. In half an hour's time I'm taking the helicopter to Azura.'

'To see Rita?' Luisa whirled round. 'Take me with you.'

There was a moment of silence. The dark eyes drove through her. Then in a quiet tone, liberally laced with menace, he put to her, 'I thought you weren't supposed to know where Rita was?'

She could have told him about the letter. She could easily have explained herself. But suddenly it felt more satisfying to hand him this apparent proof that he'd been right, that all along she had been lying to him and deceiving him.

For she could see that, after all, he had doubted his judgement. Let him too now feel what it was to be betrayed!

She said, 'I was lying.' And she smiled as his gaze shifted. 'But what does that matter? Just let me come with you.'

'I don't think I want to do that. If you want to go, find your own way.' His face had closed like a fist against her.

Luisa took a step forward. 'Don't be silly,' she told him. 'I know where she is... She's at the Beachside Hotel. If you take me with you, I'll be out of your hair that much sooner. After all, it would be pointless now for me to return to the yacht. And once I'm gone, you can relax again and call off your spies.'

'That's a comforting thought.' He smiled without humour. 'But why should I do you any favours?'

'It would be better than leaving me here alone on the yacht. After all, I might manage to give the slip to your spies... Then who knows...? I might get up to all sorts of mischief.'

'I doubt that.' His gaze was steely. 'My men are extremely well trained.'

As he fixed her with a look, Luisa felt her spirits sink. If he refused, how would she make it to Azura on her own? She had no money, no credit cards, no traveller's cheques, nothing. And suddenly she was filled with the overwhelming conviction that it was important for her to get to Rita as soon as possible. Certainly no later than Roth did. Otherwise, there might well be a disaster.

But by now she knew him well enough not to beg. Taking a chance, she turned away. 'Very well, then. Perhaps, after all, it might be more in my interests to stick around here and take advantage of your absence.'

She had almost reached the wooden staircase that led down to the lower deck. Her steps echoed behind her. I've blown it, she was thinking.

Then, as she reached for the handrail, about to descend, her heart stopped in her chest.

'OK, I'll take you,' he said.

It was the first time Luisa had ever flown in a helicopter. And, had it not been for the unhappy circumstances, she would have loved every minute.

Up there in that tiny shell, on the narrow seat beside Roth, she gazed down in fascination at the sweep of shimmering seascape, every shade of blue it was possible to imagine, and found herself wondering at the beauty of it all.

Who would ever have thought that she would be in this place, in the exotic Bahamas, flying in a private helicopter? Even just a week ago she'd never have dreamed it was possible.

But, really, she reflected, there was little to feel so thrilled about. It was a personal tragedy that had brought her here. Her sister's tragedy. And now she was about to come face to face with it.

She'd tried asking Roth before they'd set off what the purpose was of his flight to Azura.

'Why are you going to see Rita? Has something happened to her?'

He'd barely bothered to answer her. 'Not as far as I know.'

But she'd insisted. 'I take it it's not for a reconciliation? Even you, surely, don't need two women in your life?'

And the redhead, though she did not say so, out of respect for her sister, really was more his type than Rita. Just that brief glimpse of her as she'd descended from the helicopter before throwing herself joyfully into Roth's arms had been all the evidence she'd needed of that. She was sophisticated, beautiful, glamorous, made to measure.

But where was she now? Luisa had asked him that as well. 'Where's the redhead?' she'd enquired, as they'd climbed aboard the helicopter. 'What's the matter? Isn't she coming with us?'

When he hadn't deigned to answer, Luisa had drawn her own conclusions. It made sense, after all. It would be a little tacky, even for Roth, to bring along his new girlfriend to participate in the demise of the old one. For that, she was growing certain, was precisely what was about to happen.

Rita was about to receive the final formal brush-off.

Thank heavens I'm going to be there, she had decided, her heart twisting. Poor Rita was going to need all the comfort she could get. That letter to Roth had probably been begging him to reconsider and now he was about to deliver his answer in person. Thank heavens she would be there to offer a shoulder to cry on.

It was only a twenty-minute journey. Already they were over Azura, a bright green jewel in the crushed sapphire sea. In a wide sweeping curve the helicopter started to descend.

'This isn't the right hotel!'

As they came in to land, Luisa glimpsed the name of the hotel on whose roof they were about to set down. She turned to Roth and frowned. 'Rita's hotel is the Beachside.'

'Yes, I'm aware of that.' He stepped down on to the roof in front of her, slinging his weekend bag over his shoulder. 'But this is where I'll be staying. You can stay where you like.'

'Naturally, I'll stay with Rita.' Very pointedly she ignored the helping hand he was reaching out to her. 'And, what's more, I intend to go straight there.'

'Don't worry, I'll be going with you.' He was striding across the roof, heading for the door that led inside. 'I want to get this over and done with as quickly as possible.'

Callous bastard! Luisa hurried after him, clutching her plastic bag of toiletries, the only piece of luggage she'd brought with her, in spite of Roth's instructions to bring everything. All those beautiful outfits he'd spent a king's ransom on only yesterday were hanging, spurned and rejected, in her cabin wardrobe, waiting for the charity auction.

She glared at his back, despising him, hating him. 'I know what you're about to do, but I hope you plan on doing it kindly. Rita's not just a piece of junk, you know, for you to use and throw away!'

He swung round in the doorway, so that she almost walked into him. His eyes were hard. 'You seem to know a lot. So, tell me, what am I planning to do?'

'You're going to give her the elbow.' Her eyes flared back at him. 'Not to put too fine a point on it.'

'And isn't that what you want? You ought to be rejoicing.'

'I suppose it is what I want.' But she was far from rejoicing. 'What I want for my sister is for her to be happy, and I know she could never be happy with you. The best thing in the end is for her to return to her family.' She paused and bit her lip. 'But I don't want her to be hurt. Please,' she added in a softer tone, 'be as kind as you can with her.'

'I'll do my best.' He turned away impatiently. Clearly, being kind was not a major priority. All he cared about was getting Rita off his hands so that he could get back, as soon as possible, to his redhead!

He led her inside, then down a narrow staircase and finally through a pair of wide swing-doors into an astonishingly beautiful reception area hung with gilt-framed mirrors and crystal chandeliers.

No wonder, Luisa reflected, her sister wasn't staying here! A hotel like this would cost a month's wages for one night!

Roth wasted no time. Down in Reception he checked in quickly, handed his weekend bag to a porter, then strode outside to hail a taxi. Within seconds they were on their way to the Beachside Hotel.

It was a rather more modest establishment than the one they'd just left. More the sort of place Luisa was used to staying in. But she was nervous as she walked into the lobby behind Roth and stood beside him at the reception desk.

What would happen now? She dreaded to think. Her tight, anxious heart went out to her sister.

'We've come to see Mrs Browning. This young lady is her sister.' Roth nodded briefly in Luisa's direction. 'Would you kindly ring her room and let her know we're here?'

But the receptionist shook his head as he glanced up at where the keys were kept. 'I'm afraid she's out. She handed in her room key a couple of hours ago.'

'But she's still registered here? She hasn't actually checked out?'

'No, she hasn't checked out. I expect she'll be back quite soon now. She doesn't usually stay out for long.'

'Then we'll wait. And in the meantime, you can check her sister in.' Roth glanced at his watch with a quick scowl of impatience. He really grudges her every minute, Luisa thought with disapproval. He's about to break her heart and all he cares about is wasting time.

As it turned out, he was obliged to waste a considerable amount of time. Four hours later there was still no sign of Rita.

Roth and Luisa had snatched a quick, silent lunch in the little restaurant, briefly breaking their vigil in the lobby, and now it was well after three o'clock and both of them were starting to wilt a little.

'I'm going back to my hotel for a shower,' Roth announced suddenly, glancing down at his watch for at least the hundredth time. 'I'll be back in an hour. If she comes while I'm gone, make sure she stays here. Don't let her go off again.'

'Don't worry, I won't.' Luisa scowled at him angrily, as he rose to his feet and strode off across the lobby.

With every minute that passed she was growing more nervous and hating Roth more for having caused this mess in the first place. In her mind she had been going through those letters Alan had shown her, those letters so full of love and desperation. Rita was going to be shattered to learn that the affair was finally over.

Roth was back within the hour, but there was still no sign of Rita. As he appeared in the hotel doorway, Luisa was pacing the lobby.

'Where can she be?' She turned on him almost accusingly. 'Maybe she knows you're here. Maybe she's afraid to face you.'

But Roth was no comfort. His eyes were hard as he looked back at her. 'I don't know where she is any more than you do. Let me remind you I'm not your sister's keeper.'

'You bastard!'

If they had not been in a public place, Luisa might very well have hit him. Instead, stiff with emotion, she turned away sharply and, to keep herself from screaming, resumed her pacing.

Where *was* Rita? she asked herself. Had something happened to her?

Hours later it had grown dark and they were still waiting—though Luisa, unable to bear being in the tiny lobby any longer, had stepped outside to take a breath of fresh air.

There were gardens, leading to the beach, at the front of the hotel. She strolled restlessly along the pathways, one eye fixed on the hotel entrance, listening for taxis, footsteps, anything. And, inside her, her fear was growing into panic.

Something terrible had happened. Some dreadful tragedy. Her fists clenched and unclenched. She was absolutely sure of it.

Then she heard a sudden noise on the gravel behind her. She swung round, her heart spinning. 'Rita?' she cried.

But it wasn't Rita. She fell back, almost weeping, as Roth came towards her, dark hair gleaming in the moonlight.

'Are you all right?' He stopped in front of her. 'I think maybe I ought to take you to the bar for a drink.'

'I don't want a drink! How can you even suggest it?' Suddenly, something seemed to snap inside her. She lunged towards Roth, fists flailing at his chest. 'How can you talk of having a cosy drink together when my sister could be lying somewhere dead?'

'Dead? What the devil are you talking about?' He caught her by the wrists and held her firm as she continued to beat the air with her fists. 'Why on earth would your sister be dead?'

'She might have killed herself! But you don't care, do you? My sister's lying dead somewhere because of you, and you want to go to the bar for a drink!'

She was over the top now and she knew it, but she could not help herself. Suddenly Luisa was sobbing, tears streaming down her face, as she struggled and twisted and beat the air with her fists.

'Calm down. Calm down.'

Suddenly he was taking hold of her, folding her against him, his arms around her, gossamer-soft. His breath was in her hair. 'Please calm down, Luisa. I promise you your sister isn't dead.'

'How can you know that?' Her tear-stained face looked up at him. 'How can you know she isn't dead?'

'I just know it. Believe me.'

His hand caressed her back, soothing her as though she were a frightened, exhausted child. Luisa leaned against him, feeling the panic slowly leave her. She looked up at him again. 'Are you really sure?'

He smiled a gentle smile. 'I'm sure, Luisa. You have nothing to fear. I promise you that.'

His eyes in the moonlight were as dark as the universe, flooding into her, reaching down to touch her soul. And as he bent to touch the tip of her nose with a fleeting kiss she sighed and closed her eyes. There was nothing to fear.

But then a harsh voice suddenly broke the silence.

'Am I interrupting something?'

She jerked round to see Rita.

CHAPTER EIGHT

'THANK God you're safe!'

As she spun round to face Rita, the words burst spontaneously from Luisa's lips. A rush of relief went pouring through her. 'I was so worried when we didn't find you here. I was starting to imagine all sorts of things!'

'Is that so? How very touching. But, from the looks of things, I'd say the one in danger was you.'

Glittering in her tight face, Rita's eyes swept over Luisa—then over Roth who, though he had dropped his arms away, was still standing by her side. Her lips thinned with white fury. 'This was the last thing I'd expected. You didn't waste much time, did you, little sister?'

'Oh, but it's not how it looks!'

Appalled, Luisa stepped towards her, deliberately distancing herself from Roth. Through her relief, suddenly she was filled with burning guilt and confusion. 'I was upset...about you. Roth was comforting me. That was all.'

'Yes, I'll bet!' Rita's tone was chipped ice. 'I'll bet that's all that Roth was doing!' Then her cheeks suddenly flared with hectic colour. 'How could you?' she screamed. She stepped towards her threateningly. 'My own sister! How could you? You filthy rotten tramp!'

Luisa had been prepared for this reaction. Her excuse, after all, even to her own ears, had sounded pathetic and barely credible. Though, why should it? she told herself. It was perfectly true.

She frowned at Rita. 'Please don't get upset. I promise you, there's nothing to get upset about.'

'No? Just look at these clothes you're wearing!' Suddenly, Rita's eyes alighted on the chic designer outfit. '*He* bought those for you, didn't he? Payment for services rendered!'

'Rita, that's not true...!' Luisa felt mortified. 'Rita, I promise you, you've got it all wrong!'

But Rita wasn't listening to her. Instead she was lunging at her, grabbing her by the hair, screeching like a banshee, nails like a cat's claws flying for her face.

And that was when Roth stepped forward and took over.

'That's enough.' He grabbed each of them by the shoulder and yanked them apart as though they were puppets. Then, still holding them apart, he decreed in a firm tone, 'We'll go back to the hotel, have ourselves a drink, and discuss this whole thing in a civilised manner. I've no desire to take part in a public brawl.'

'No, you wouldn't, would you?' Rita's lips curled sneeringly. But suddenly she had grown still as Roth continued to hold her—as though the touch of him had frozen something inside her.

She made an effort to shrug his hand away as she glared balefully into his face. 'You can do what you like, but I'm tired and I'm going to bed. I'm not in the mood for one of your little discussions.

Between you and your bloody sister, I've had all the discussions I can stomach.'

'Sister?' Involuntarily, the question slipped from Luisa's lips. She glanced at Roth, a frown on her face.

A fleeting smile touched his lips. 'The redhead, remember?'

'You mean she really was your sister?' Luisa blinked back at him foolishly. And though it was utterly inappropriate for the moment, she felt a sudden warmth go through her as he nodded his affirmation. Then she snatched her eyes away. What difference did it make?

Rita was standing, gaze downcast, staring at the ground. She said in a dull tone, 'Let go of me, Roth. I'm tired. I want to go to bed.'

His hand remained on her shoulder. 'Very well,' he agreed. 'But I shall be back for that little discussion of ours tomorrow morning, bright and early. I haven't come all this way for nothing.'

'Do what you like. You always do, don't you?' Rita's tone was hostile, but flat and weary. Clearly, there was no more violence left in her. As Roth released her, she turned away, heading for the hotel entrance. She had not even glanced at Luisa.

'I'll come with you.' Luisa began to hurry after her. 'I'll see you to your room. I'll——'

'Kindly don't bother.' Rita glared at her with malice over her shoulder. 'I can find my own way to my room. I don't need any help from you.'

'Please, Rita.' Luisa felt chilled by the look in Rita's eyes. 'I just want to see that you're OK.'

'Why, are you afraid I might do something foolish, little sister?' Rita's tone was scornful. Then she added viciously, 'That would be nasty for you, wouldn't it? People would say it was all your fault.'

'But, Rita——'

'Just leave me!' Rita had turned away again. 'Go back to your lover and finish what I interrupted!'

Luisa felt torn in two. As Rita swept towards the door, she paused, then changed her mind and started to hurry after her again. 'Rita, please... I'm concerned for you, that's all.'

'Don't waste your concern.'

It was Roth who'd spoken suddenly, coming up behind her, making her jump. As Luisa started and turned round, he added, 'Forget it. Let her go. What we all need now is a good night's sleep. We can continue this little farce in the morning.'

'Farce', he called it, standing there so cool and superior. He really didn't care. None of it had touched him.

'How can you?' Suddenly, Luisa was filled with anger against him. 'How can you be so utterly unfeeling? You're the one who's to blame for all this! If anything happens to my sister, it'll be your fault!'

Callously, he shrugged. 'If anything happens to your sister, it'll be your sister's fault. She's a grown, adult woman. She knows what she's doing.'

Luisa turned away. His lack of caring was shocking. 'Damn you!' she muttered. 'I'm going after her!' Then she was hurrying up the path to the hotel entrance, almost running across the lobby, heading for the lifts.

She reached Rita's room just as Rita was stepping through the door. An instant later, the door slammed in her face.

Luisa knew she wouldn't sleep. She paced her room for over an hour, pausing from time to time to step out on to the tiny balcony and gaze down at the shadowy, moonlit beach. Her brain felt as though at any minute it might burst.

What a day it had been. And what a night. She felt wrung out emotionally, as limp as a rag. Desperately, she struggled to make sense of all that had happened.

Basically, what had happened was that things were in a worse mess than before! Not only was there the tragedy of Rita and Roth to contend with, but there was the added disaster that Rita now believed that there was something going on between Luisa and Roth.

The whole thing was like some evil witch's brew that just grew more potent and dangerous the more you stirred it!

And it's all my fault, Luisa told herself, as she gazed out from the balcony. If I hadn't got in such a state about Rita, Roth wouldn't have had to comfort me and none of this would have happened.

She thought back to the afternoon and the way she had succumbed to her anxiety. It was natural for her to have been worried—she did care about Rita—but it wasn't like her to get so hopelessly wound up like that. After all, she reminded herself, why was I getting so upset at the prospect of Roth breaking off the affair when it was precisely in the hope of putting an end to it that I came to the Bahamas in the first place?

It just didn't make any sense. Or did it?

Luisa frowned up at the moon. I know what happened, she admitted, feeling uncomfortable as she forced herself to face the truth. What happened was that I was putting myself in Rita's place. I was imagining how *I* would feel if that were to happen to me.

She sighed and shook her head. It was mad but it was true. By some trick of the psyche she'd suddenly understood how it would feel to be in love with Roth.

It would be an emotion, she'd known with certainty, of totally consuming magnitude. It would possess one heart and body and soul. It would be a love the like of which the world could scarcely imagine. Blinding, hypnotic, a terrible, wonderful thing.

And to be suddenly faced with the rejection of such a love would be a blow more dreadful than any heart could cope with. One's life would be blighted, one's soul crushed forever.

And thinking of the dreadful hurt that lay in store for Rita, Luisa had found herself reacting as though the victim were herself. That was what had unravelled her composure and brought on that fit of near-hysteria. She'd been feeling and hurting and suffering as though she were Rita. It was a puzzling, frightening thing, but that was what had happened.

And, in the end, these feelings had been misplaced, she'd discovered. The affair, it would appear, had already been over. And though her sister was clearly distraught, Luisa had sensed very strongly that Rita was far from crushed by the blow. The emotions that had sprung from her were anger and resentment. Her heart was more filled with hatred than with pain.

That was probably good, Luisa decided, breathing in the night air, struggling to shake off the disquietude that still clung to her. It was better that her sister was simply angry, not suicidal, as at one point she had seriously feared she might be. Anger was healthy when channelled openly and positively. Luisa didn't even really mind that some of it was currently channelled against her!

She sighed. Though I shall put her right on that point first thing tomorrow morning! I shall assure her that there's nothing going on between Roth and me!

Luisa turned away from the balcony and resumed her pacing. It was hopeless. She felt like a caged tiger in this room. She glanced at her watch. It was just after ten. Perhaps a walk along the beach might help her to unwind.

A moment later, room key in hand, she was hurrying downstairs. Then she was striding through the door that led out to the gardens and down to the silvery stretch of beach beyond. Her steps were quick and light. The key jangled in her hand.

There was no one about as she kicked off her sandals and, slinging them in one hand, set off along the beach. She breathed in deeply. Already, she felt better!

The sand was cool against her feet, trickling between her toes. She relaxed her shoulders, shrugging off her tension. A brisk walk and then she would go back and try to sleep.

But she had gone not more than half a dozen metres when a voice behind her made her start.

'Do you mind if I join you?' it asked.

Luisa swung round, very nearly dropping her sandals. 'What do you think you're doing? You almost gave me a heart attack!'

'Sorry. I didn't mean to.'

Roth was standing a few feet away. He was dressed in light trousers and an open-neck blue shirt, rolled back casually to the elbows. Luisa's heart thumped violently as she looked into his face.

'So, do you mind if I join you? I think we ought to have a chat.'

'A chat?' Luisa squinted into his face. Beneath the pale silvery moonlight his hair looked very dark, and his eyes, as they watched her, seemed endlessly deep and black. Just for an instant she felt mesmerised by those eyes.

She shook the feeling from her. 'I don't think I fancy a chat.' Suddenly, just his presence was making her feel edgy. 'I came down here to try and unwind,' she told him crisply. 'Somehow I don't think one of your chats would help that process.'

Roth shrugged. 'OK, if you prefer, we won't chat. I'll just join you for a quiet little stroll.'

I don't fancy that either. The words went through her head. But she did not say them. Instead, she turned away. Instead, she said, 'Suit yourself.'

Luisa could feel him following behind her, his footsteps light in the soft sand. And though she wanted to feel irritated, she was aware that she did not. She actually felt quite pleased in a puzzled sort of way.

And she knew she shouldn't feel that way. She said with an edge of censure, 'How come you knew I was here? And what are you doing here anyway? You ought to be at your own hotel, not hanging around here.'

He had come alongside her, and she was suddenly intensely aware of his tall muscular figure striding at her side. He seemed to blot out everything else around them. The beach. The sky. The sea. The moon.

He told her, 'I came to see if you were all right... and because I was hoping for a chance to chat. I didn't ring you because I thought you might be asleep, but I was hoping I might find you in the dining-room or somewhere. I was just about to leave when I saw you come down here.'

Bad timing on my part! She thought the words, but again didn't say them. Instead, she simply said, 'I see.' It was silly, but she felt rather glad that he had found her. There was something rather pleasant about walking with him in the moonlight, in spite of the edgy way he made her feel. It was a nice kind of edgy. Almost exciting.

As she wrestled with that thought, it struck her, too, that she was suddenly curious to know what he'd been wanting to chat about—though some sixth sense held her back from asking. It would be wiser, it seemed to be warning her, to steer clear of that subject.

They walked along in silence for a moment. And as Luisa stared down at the sand, she found herself observing that her feet and Roth's were moving in perfect easy rhythm, as though the two sets of feet were powered by one mind. It reminded her of those other times when they had seemed so physically in unison, when every move made by one of them seemed to echo the other, and suddenly, as in the past, the feeling discomfited her.

Deliberately, she upset the rhythm between them, shortening her steps so they no longer coincided with his. She said, seeking to strengthen this reassuring disharmony, 'I hope that, like me, you're going to assure Rita tomorrow that she's wrong in her assumptions about you and me? Heaven knows where she could have got such a notion in the first place!'

Luisa felt him smile. 'Heaven knows,' he agreed.

She turned sharply to look at him. 'And what is that supposed to mean?'

'It means I couldn't agree with you more.'

He continued to smile at her, an amused, taunting smile that for some reason had caused Luisa's skin to prickle strangely. She snatched her gaze away as, suddenly, out of nowhere, as vivid as though it had happened a mere moment ago, came a memory of that moment before Rita had caught them together.

She could feel his arms around her and herself sinking against his chest. She could feel his lips brushing the tip of her nose. And she could feel, too, the way her heart had pressed inside her chest.

Had he been doing more than just comforting her? she suddenly wondered. And had she been seeking more than just comfort?

The thought seemed almost indecent. Luisa rejected it, violently. How could anything like that have passed between them when surely all that had been in her mind at that time was Rita? It could not be! It was base and shocking!

She focused on Rita now as she turned to deliver him a sharp glance. 'Why did you come here to see Rita?' she put to him. 'It was to finally put an end to things between you, wasn't it? You'd obviously already tried, but this time you were going to be more ruthless.'

He had stopped. He was no longer walking alongside her. It took Luisa a moment or two to realise it. Then she stopped too and turned on him accusingly.

'What's the matter?' she challenged him. 'Am I a little too close to the truth?'

'You're miles from the truth.'

'You mean you weren't going to be ruthless?' Her tone was mocking. 'Don't tell me you were going to be kind?'

He took a deep breath, his gaze driving into her, as he stood there, stock-still, in the moonlight. In a flat tone he said, 'There was never an affair.'

'Never an affair!' Luisa laughed out loud. 'Is that supposed to be a joke or what?'

'There was never an affair.' As he repeated his statement, Luisa felt the smile fall from her face. 'If you'll give me a chance,' he was saying, 'I'll tell you what really happened.'

There was something in his expression that compelled her attention. Luisa nodded and regarded him mutely as he continued,

'Your sister has been a thorn in my side for many months. It all started when I was involved in negotiations with her husband regarding the take-over of his company. We had dinner together a couple of times—all three of us,' he stressed meaningfully. 'Then on several occasions I was invited round to their house.'

He smiled a grim smile. 'It soon became very clear that your sister had what you might call designs on me. I did my best to rebuff them without alerting her husband. But she persisted. I was bombarded with phone calls and letters, even the occasional indiscreet visit to my hotel room.

'Nothing happened. Not one kiss passed between us.' He paused and looked into Luisa's startled, wide-eyed face. 'I mean no disrespect whatsoever to your sister, but she's really not my type. I wasn't remotely tempted.'

Then he pulled a face. 'But in spite of that, in spite of the fact that she received no encouragement, she kept up her pursuit throughout the time I was in Yorkshire. I thought it would stop when I left, but alas I was wrong about that. She followed me all the way to the Bahamas...'

As he paused, Luisa just stared at him, suddenly speechless. She felt she ought to be rejecting what he was saying, but to her horror it sounded remarkably like the truth. Hadn't she herself always thought that Rita was hardly Roth's type?

All she could think of to say was, 'Why didn't you tell me this before?'

'Would you have believed me?'

'No, I suppose I wouldn't.' And she wasn't really sure why she believed him now. All she knew was that she did. Absolutely. There was no need for him to say, as he took a step towards her,

'If you need proof, I have stacks of letters I can show you. At first, I destroyed them all. They were merely hysterical and silly, but I decided to hang on to them when they started to become more threatening.'

Again he paused, and his tone had altered as he added, 'But then you know all about that bit already, don't you?'

For a moment, still stunned, Luisa looked back at him in bafflement. Then the penny dropped. 'You mean about the book? About the stories she was going to tell people about you? You mean she sent you letters, threatening to do that?'

'Foolish of her, wasn't it? Rather self-defeating. I don't suppose you knew about the letters?'

'It would seem I didn't know anything about any of it!' Shocked, Luisa sank to her knees in the sand. 'You mean this whole affair never happened? That it was just an invention of my sister's? That she left her husband and her children for something that wasn't even real?'

'It was an obsession, a fixation. The psychologists have names for it. And I'm sure at times she almost convinced herself it *was* real. Certainly, her hatred for me at my rejection of her was real enough. And so was the effect she's had on my life. The past few weeks since she came out here have been a nightmare.'

Luisa had laid aside her sandals and room key on the sand. Suddenly, the world had turned topsy-turvy. The victim had become a villain and the villain a victim. Her heart went out to Roth for what he must have suffered.

She looked up into his face as he continued to look down at her. 'Why didn't you report her—or at least tell her husband?'

'I was close to doing both.' He sighed and sank down beside her. 'But I was reluctant to do either for fear of making trouble for her and maybe breaking up her marriage. At heart, I believe your sister's a decent woman. I've seen her with her children and I know she's a good mother. I was just hoping that one day—preferably soon—she'd wake up finally recovered from her brainstorm and go back to Yorkshire and get on with her life.'

'I'll bet you were! It must have been dreadful!' Filled with sympathy for him, Luisa leaned towards him. 'Most men wouldn't have been half so patient.'

'I don't know if patient's the right word.' He stretched his long legs out in front of him. 'There were times when I came very close to homicide. That was how my sister got involved—after Rita gatecrashed the party. She was afraid I might end up doing something drastic!'

So, her eyes had not deceived her! She *had* seen Rita at the party! Though, clearly, she had not been allowed to stay long!

Luisa looked into Roth's face, aware of a warmth rushing through her. For at last she was seeing him for what he really was—a warm, humane and deeply caring man, and to a degree way beyond all normal expectation.

How many other men in his situation would have held back from claiming the protection they had a right to out of a fear of breaking up their tormentor's family? Very few, she decided. He was one in a million.

Regret poured through her as she frowned into his eyes. How hopelessly, how cruelly, she had misjudged him!

'Anita—my sister,' he was continuing, 'flew out here to Azura to try to talk to her. We thought maybe a woman could talk some sense into her. But she had no more success than I'd had,' he added, frowning. 'That was why I decided to have one more try myself.' He caught Luisa's eye. 'So, now you know why I'm here.'

'Quite a story.' Luisa shook her head. And as she looked at him, though it was ridiculous, she longed to reach out and embrace him. She longed to express with more than just words how sorry she was.

'But it's over now, I promise you.' Her expression was serious. 'And there's no need for you to be involved any longer. I'm going to get hold of that sister of mine first tomorrow morning and, one way or another, I'm going to talk some sense into her. And then I'm going to personally accompany her on the first flight back to England.'

'Are you, now?' Roth had leaned towards her suddenly. He reached out and flicked a strand of hair behind her shoulder. 'It sounds to me as though you've suddenly changed sides.'

'I would have changed sides long ago if I'd known what was going on!' A shiver went through her as his hand brushed against her ear. 'Why didn't you tell me all this from the start?'

'Because you were the enemy. One doesn't confide in the enemy.'

'Why was I the enemy?' Luisa gazed at him, perplexed. How could I be the enemy, she was thinking, when I love you?

The thought stopped her in her tracks. Surely not? she told herself. But her heart was telling her differently as he moved a little closer.

'You were the enemy,' he was saying softly, 'because you were against me.'

Yes, she had been against him. Her heart was pounding. It seemed impossible to believe now. She reached out to him and shook her head.

'Don't you want to be my enemy any more?'

He caught her hand and held it, the dark eyes only inches from her face. Then, as she murmured, 'Oh, no... I don't want to be your enemy...' the hand that had brushed her ear slid round to the back of her neck. A shiver went through her as his fingers tangled in her hair.

Luisa could hear the blood pounding like an earthquake in her brain. As he drew her even closer, dry-mouthed, she told him, 'It seems silly now... I mean that I could ever have been against you.'

'Silly and sad.' His eyes poured into her. He kissed her hand softly then slipped his arm round her waist. 'I wish it were possible that we had never been enemies.'

But that's all over now. Luisa gazed back at him, overwhelmed by the feelings that were pouring through her.

I *do* love him, she admitted. I love him and I want him more than I've ever wanted anyone or anything in my life.

And she knew, as he gazed down at her, that he wanted her, too. She could almost feel their two hearts moving in step together, the wanting and the needing in them in perfect united rhythm. She let out a cry of sheer joy as at last he bent to kiss her.

Instantly, as his lips covered hers, she was alight, her entire body responding to his touch the way a bomb responded to the touch of a lighted paper. An explosion tore through her as she gasped and shuddered against him, her hands reaching out with a sigh to caress his face.

They had fallen back into the sand. Suddenly, Luisa was flat on her back and Roth was half lying, half leaning over her. She could feel the welcome weight of him. She could feel his vibrant hardness. Her arms twined around his neck, drawing him closer.

'My beautiful, desirable enemy!'

His hands caressed her, sweeping down her flanks, causing a melting deep inside her, as they pushed up her skirt to allow him access to her thighs. And as they swept round to caress her buttocks, tangling briefly with her panties, she tensed, half expecting him to pull the lacy briefs away.

And she would not have stopped him. She would not have stopped him doing anything. At that moment, more than willingly, she would have surrendered to him totally.

But he drew his hand away and adjusted her skirt again, then raised himself a little to gaze down into her face.

'My wickedly desirable enemy...'

His hand caressed her face, then slid down past her shoulder to linger against her breast. As he grazed the hard peak, she felt a shiver go through her. Her body seemed to slacken and tighten at the same time. Every inch of her was crying out for his possession.

He continued to look down at her as his hand caressed her, circling her breast slowly, almost distractedly, sending fire through her loins, making her insane.

She sighed. 'Roth!' And reached out to him. But that was when he drew away.

Suddenly, inexplicably, he was rising to his feet, then reaching down to take her hand and drawing her up alongside him. He bent down to gather up her sandals and keys from the sand and handed them to her, saying, 'I'll take you back to the hotel now.'

'But why?'

She couldn't stop it. She couldn't hold the question back. Luisa looked into his face. 'Why?' she asked again.

'Because, once, you were my enemy.' He looked straight at her, and her heart froze to see how his expression had hardened. 'And that,' he added, moving away from her, 'is something we can never change.'

At first, as she followed him back across the sand, Luisa simply felt numb, all feeling gone. She didn't even try to understand what he'd meant. But by the time they'd reached the garden and were approaching the hotel entrance, it was as though a floodlight had switched on in her brain. Suddenly, she understood with perfect clarity.

He still believed, of course, that she had plotted against him! She had not told him that that was a lie, like all the rest!

'Roth!' As they arrived at the door and he was about to take his leave of her, she reached out to lay a hand on his arm. 'Roth, please wait a minute. I have something to tell you.' Her heart was spilling over with excitement inside her.

But then she froze again as he turned to face her, his expression dark, his eyes harsh and forbidding.

'The only thing I want you to tell me,' he gritted, 'is that you meant it when you said that you're going to talk to your sister and get her on the first plane back to England. Frankly, I've had all I can stand of both of you. If you're still here on Azura by tomorrow night, I'll report you both to the authorities!'

The harsh words fell like a sword between them. There was a shiver and a seemingly endless silence. Then, in a small voice Luisa told him, 'Take my word, I meant it. We'll both be gone from here long before tomorrow night.'

Then, helplessly, she was watching him stride off into the darkness, suddenly feeling as though some giant mailed fist had reached down from the sky and crushed her.

CHAPTER NINE

'How will you ever be able to forgive me?'

It wasn't until they were actually on the plane, heading out of Nassau back to London, that Rita broke down in tears of remorse. Back on Azura that morning, throughout Luisa's kindly but stern lecture—the one she'd promised Roth she'd deliver—Rita had remained silent, her face devoid of all emotion. It was only when Luisa had finished speaking that she'd raised her eyes and said simply, 'I'll come with you.'

Luisa had sighed with relief. She had expected a battle. She'd half expected to have to drag her sister on to the plane. And in her current state of mind she was in no mood for more trauma. Her final parting with Roth had been trauma enough.

But there had been no more trauma. Rita had gone like a lamb. By mid-afternoon they were heading for Nassau to pick up their international flight to London—Luisa stopping off in Nassau just long enough to make a dash to her hotel and pick up her things.

She'd felt a sense of relief as she'd changed into her own clothes and changed some traveller's cheques to pay Rita back the money she'd lent her. I'm me again, she'd told herself, in charge of my life again. I'm not that silly vulnerable creature who thought she was in love with Roth Elman.

The illusion had been bolstered as she handed into hotel reception, carefully wrapped, the designer outfit she'd been wearing and told the receptionist, 'Please donate these to some local charity.' Of that silly vulnerable creature there was not a trace left.

No *visible* trace, perhaps. But deep in her heart throbbed a pain that would not be so easily disposed of. She was going to miss Roth. There was no doubt about it. And she had a nasty suspicion that from now on she would spend her life comparing other men to him. And every man she compared to him would inevitably come out wanting.

Luisa tried to squash these feelings. She barely knew him, she told herself. He was a mere, fleeting illusion who had flashed briefly through her life.

But she knew that meant nothing. In that brief time she'd known him he'd turned her life upside-down and her heart inside out. He'd left her forever changed. And hopelessly in love.

Hopelessly.

As she and Rita climbed on board the plane, Luisa forced herself to focus on that thought. For that was precisely what her love was, a love without hope. So she must do the only sane thing. She must try to forget it.

She'd turned to look at Rita as they'd buckled themselves into their seats. It was almost funny. They were both in the same boat. Both in love with the same man, a man whom neither of them could ever have. Suddenly, she felt closer to Rita than perhaps she had ever done before.

It was just after they'd taken off that Rita suddenly turned to her. She laid a hand on Luisa's arm and started to speak.

'Luisa, I'm so sorry. I'm so ashamed of everything. I don't know what came over me. I've been behaving like a madwoman.'

Luisa looked into her face that suddenly looked pale and strained. 'Yes, you have rather,' she agreed kindly. 'But it's over now. Don't be too hard on yourself.'

'How can I not be too hard? The way I behaved was awful! When I think of it, I want to die!' Tears were streaming down her face.

Luisa took her hand in hers as, between sobs and tears, Rita proceeded to pour out the whole messy story—almost word for word as Roth had recounted it last night.

'It was an obsession I couldn't control,' Rita ended, drying her eyes. 'It wasn't really love. It was just some kind of madness. And I knew it was madness.' She gave a shaky laugh. 'Can you imagine a man like Roth ever being interested in someone like me?'

Before Luisa could answer, she hurried on, surprising her, 'You're more his type. No, I mean it. Really. I thought that last night when I saw you together.' She held Luisa's gaze, but without any sign of anger. '*Is* there something going on between you?'

Luisa felt a dart of pain, but fought to hide it. 'Of course not,' she answered. 'Anyway, I already told you what he thinks of me! He thinks I was the dreaded biographer you threatened him with!'

'I'm sorry about that.' Rita's face puckered with shame. 'I never intended to get you mixed up in this.' Then she squeezed Luisa's hand. 'I'm so grateful to you, Luisa, for going to all the trouble you went to, coming out to fetch me. I've been wanting to come back for a couple of weeks, but I was so confused I just didn't seem to know what I was doing.'

'It was no trouble. I'm just happy that it all turned out right and that now you're going back to get on with your old life again.'

'Yes, isn't that wonderful!' A smile lit Rita's face. 'I could hardly believe it when Alan told me on the phone this morning that he forgives me for everything and wants me back again.' Her voice broke. 'I couldn't have borne to lose him or my children. I love them so much. I must have been crazy.'

As more tears threatened, Luisa smiled at her mock-sternly. 'It's all over now. You ought to be celebrating, not weeping. Come on, let's have a drink,' she suggested cheerfully. 'How about a bottle of champagne? Let's drink to the future and forget about the past.'

But as the stewardess brought the champagne and the two sisters raised their glasses, Luisa was suddenly filled with a sense of fearful sadness.

What future could she look forward to when she would never see Roth again? And how could she forget a past she knew would haunt her forever?

'Merrylegs, come here and stop all that barking!'

Luisa laughed as she called to the yapping little dog who was running excitedly across the garden.

'There's nobody there. Come and sit down here beside me.'

For once, the little dog did as he was told and came bounding across the grass towards her, tail wagging frantically, and collapsed at her feet. Luisa tickled his ears. 'That's better,' she told him. 'You must learn only to bark when there's some stranger there to bark at.'

Then she smiled to herself. I'm going crazy, she thought. I spend my days talking to a dog!

It was just over four weeks since Luisa had got back from the Bahamas, though at times, she reflected, it felt more like four years. That short week she had spent there belonged to another life. A life that, every single day that went by, she had to struggle to banish from her thoughts. It was a struggle she had to admit she hadn't quite won yet, although maybe, just maybe, she was starting to get there.

Certainly, she was doing all within her power to fill her mind with other things. She had come up here to Bath to dog- and house-sit for some friends, armed with a veritable mountain of work.

There were a clutch of articles she was busily researching, another couple she was in the process of writing up, and, just in case that wasn't enough to fill her time, there was also the book for the New York publisher that she'd brought along to work on as well.

She'd been working on that now, out on the patio, as the warm August sun began to sink towards the west. And it was going well. She was making good progress. She'd felt quite justified in taking a short break for a cup of coffee.

And she'd been sitting drinking it at the edge of the garden, relaxing in one of the striped canvas chairs, when Merrylegs had suddenly started barking.

Luisa glanced down at the little dog, curled up peacefully now at her feet. She'd been here for three weeks, looking after her friends' house while they were off on holiday in Italy, and she and Merrylegs had become the best of friends. She would miss him a little when she went back to London.

At that thought her heart contracted. It was foolish, she knew that, but she was dreading the thought of going back to London.

London was normality. London was the old routine. Once she was back in London she would be forced to emerge from the feeling of unreality that still hung about her. And that feeling of unreality was her only protection.

Protection from what? Impatiently, she drank her coffee. She had cried a lot of tears, she had passed sleepless nights—particularly during her first couple of weeks back—but she was OK now. She needed no protecting. She had faced squarely and without compromise the reality that stood before her—namely a life without Roth, forever and ever. And she had accepted it. She needed no protection.

Luisa glanced at her watch, dousing the flicker of pain inside her. It was time to get back to work. Work was a great therapy. And maybe, she decided, glancing up at the sky, she could finish the section she was working on before the sun went down.

She stood up and, clearing her mind, started to walk back to the patio.

'Not much of a guard dog, is he?'

Suddenly a voice spoke, a voice she recognised instantly. Luisa whirled round disbelievingly, almost dropping her coffee-cup.

'I'm sorry I startled you.' He was walking towards her. 'I rang the front doorbell, but you obviously didn't hear it. So, I decided to take a look round the back.'

'I see. No, I didn't hear it.' Luisa was standing like a statue. Quite simply, she felt as though her entire body had frozen. Quite simply, she could not believe her eyes.

He was dressed in a blue suit, the jacket hanging open, with a plain white shirt and a toning blue tie. Against the whiteness of the shirt his skin glowed darkly—and, looking at him, she could almost feel the warmth of the Bahamas, could almost catch the tang of the sea in her nostrils.

Her heart welled up inside her. She stared hard at the grass.

'I hope I'm not interrupting.' Roth cast a glance at the little table, directly behind her, where her work lay spread out. 'Though I suspect I probably am. You were working, I see.'

'You're not really interrupting.' Luisa glanced round at the table as though she hadn't noticed it before. She felt suddenly as though she were acting in a dream, that when she turned back to look at him again he would no longer be there.

But he was. And he was saying, 'What were you doing?'

Luisa shrugged. 'Just doing a bit of work on the book.'

'The book?'

'The one I told you about.' She felt a quick, defensive spurt. Surely he didn't think she was working on his biography? 'The one I've been commissioned to do for the New York publishers.'

'Ah, yes. It's to be a collection of your interviews, as I recall?'

'That's right.' As she looked back at him, her defensiveness melted to be replaced by a fortifying sense of quiet anger. Why should she be defensive? She had never been guilty of the sin he had so unjustly accused her of. She had never intended to pry into his affairs.

Feeling a little less shell-shocked now, she looked into his face. 'Why are you here? What do you want with me?' Then a sudden thought occurred to her. 'And how did you find me?'

He smiled then. 'That wasn't easy.' Then he began to walk towards her. He stopped right in front of her, almost causing her to step back. 'It took me two and a half weeks to track you down here.'

'Two and a half weeks?' Luisa looked back at him, astonished. Why on earth would he have spent two and a half weeks looking for her?

He held her eyes, seeming to read her mind. 'As you can see, I wanted to find you pretty badly.'

'I can't think why.'

Her mind searched through the possibilities. She didn't owe him any money. She hadn't walked off with the silver. As far as she knew, they had no unfinished business whatsoever.

And she could not, *dared* not, imagine for one minute that he had gone to all this trouble for any reason that would please her. It could not be that he simply wanted to see her.

Yet, deny it as she would, the hope flared briefly inside her. That was why she could not bring herself to look him in the eye—for fear of seeing that vain hope instantly denied.

As she stared fixedly at one of his shirt buttons, she heard him say, 'Aren't you going to ask me to sit down?'

He was right, she ought to have done that long ago. Apart from anything else, such routine civilities would help her to take control of the situation. And, right now, a little control was something she badly needed.

'Of course.' She stepped aside and waved him towards the table, still nervously clutching her empty coffee-cup in her hand. 'Would you like a drink? Tea or coffee—or something stronger?'

'That's very kind of you. I wouldn't mind a coffee.'

Luisa watched him as he seated himself in one of the wicker chairs that were arranged around the little table. And it struck her suddenly that there was something changed about him. Though on the surface he seemed like the same old Roth of before, totally in command, totally self-confident, she sensed a ripple of tension beneath the surface.

He had something on his mind. Something was bothering him.

She hurried through to the kitchen with a sense of foreboding. He had something to tell her. Something unpleasant. And he was dreading telling her as much as she was suddenly dreading hearing it. That was why he was wasting time, taking a seat, accepting coffee.

She had to be right. There had to be something. For that was not normally Roth's way. Normally, he got straight to the point. Normally, he was nothing if not direct!

Luisa opened the cupboard door and stared blankly at the shelves. What awful thing could he possibly have to tell her? What trouble was he about to heap on her head?

She abandoned the cupboard—she had forgotten what she was looking for!—and instead lifted two mugs down from their hooks on the dresser. Then she filled the coffee-maker, scarcely aware of what she was doing. Her mind was suddenly going round in circles of anxiety. Why did he have to find her? Why couldn't he let her be?

She switched on the coffee-maker, then impatiently switched it off again. She had forgotten the coffee! That was what she'd needed from the cupboard!

Get a grip on yourself! She pulled the cupboard door open, lifted down the coffee tin and yanked the lid open.

'Can I give you a hand?'

Suddenly he was standing behind her. Luisa jumped, emptying the coffee tin all over the floor.

'Now look what you've done!' In dismay she stared down at the dark brown mess on the spotless tiled floor. 'I'll have to go and get a dustpan and sweep it up.'

But as she started to move away, suddenly he had taken hold of her. 'Forget the coffee. Forget the dustpan.' Gently but firmly, he drew her away from the spilled coffee. His eyes poured into her. 'I didn't come here for coffee.'

'No, I'm sure you didn't!' She tried to struggle free from him. Whatever he had come for, suddenly more strongly than ever Luisa didn't want to hear it.

'I came because I have to speak to you.'

She felt a spurt of panic. 'Well, maybe I don't want to listen to you!'

'You'll listen anyway.' He held her firmly. 'You'll listen and you'll listen good—because I've never done this before, and I want to be sure you hear every word.'

'I don't want to hear every word! I don't want to hear any of it!' She struggled again, futilely, against him.

And then suddenly he released her.

She saw him take a deep breath.

He looked into her eyes. 'I'm here to ask your forgiveness.'

'Forgiveness?'

Luisa could not believe what she'd just heard. She stared at him uncomprehendingly as he continued, 'I accused you of being my enemy, of setting out to try and spy on me.' A look of pain touched his face. 'I was wrong and I owe you an apology.'

Luisa was leaning against the counter, half wishing he was still holding her. Her legs all at once could barely support her. She said, 'So, what made you come to that conclusion?'

'My own common sense, once I'd thought about it properly—which, alas, was not until after you'd left. It was only then that I became convinced that I must be mistaken, that you just weren't capable of behaving like that...'

The look in his eyes was like a ray of sunshine, reaching out to warm her frightened, anxious heart. Yet she was afraid to embrace it. Maybe it meant nothing. She countered, accusingly, 'So, what took you so long? Why couldn't you have realised that in the first place?'

'I wish I had. I've asked myself a thousand times why I didn't realise sooner that you'd never been a spy.' Then his eyes narrowed. 'Of course, I wasn't helped by the fact that you didn't deny it——'

'Didn't deny it? I denied it from the start!' Before he could continue, Luisa cut in. 'How can you say I didn't deny it?'

He reached out and touched her arm, making her entire body shiver. 'I know. You're right. You did deny it. And I was wrong not to have believed you right from the beginning. I was being driven crazy by that business with your sister, and it all somehow seemed to fit together...' He paused. 'But there's no point in going over all that...'

He reached up and flicked a strand of hair across her shoulder. 'What I was going to say was that there was one crucial moment when you didn't deny it when you could have...' His hand brushed her ear, sending tingles of warmth through her. 'Do you remember that night on the beach?'

Remember it? She was never likely to forget it! She nodded. 'Of course.' Then she closed her eyes, suddenly feeling as though she were melting, as his hand slipped round to the back of her neck.

'You didn't deny it then... and surely that was the moment to do so... when we were at last laying everything out in the open, finally unravelling the tangle of misunderstandings.'

'I know.' She had regretted endlessly that missed opportunity. She frowned at him. 'For some reason I didn't think to, not just then, not when we were down on the beach together.' She looked into his eyes, regretfully, remembering. 'I was so overwhelmed with what you were telling me—about Rita and you, and how wrong I'd been about you—that it didn't cross my mind to deny it at that point...'

She faltered. 'It was only when we were on our way back to the hotel that it struck me that I ought to have spoken out...' She paused. 'And I was going to...'

'If I'd given you a chance, instead of turning on you the way I did.' As he finished the sentence for her, he stroked her hair gently. 'I really do have a lot to ask you to forgive me for.'

The touch of him was sending goose-bumps down her spine. But it was the look in his eyes that had caused the roaring in her head. Was she imagining the tenderness she suddenly thought she saw there?

She said, her fear rising as hope spilled within her, knowing she would not survive if all those fragile hopes were dashed now, 'Don't worry, it doesn't really matter.'

'Not matter?' All at once his hand had grown still. A dark shadow seemed to have settled in his eyes. 'Do you mean that? Doesn't it matter to you that I ask your forgiveness?'

'No, I didn't mean that.' Luisa held her breath. For a moment it had seemed he was about to step away from her. 'What I mean is you don't have to worry about my forgiving you. I already have. And there was really nothing to forgive.'

His eyes closed for a moment, then once more he gazed down at her. He sighed. 'You mean that? I really am forgiven?'

'I was as much to blame as you for everything that happened.' She smiled a shaky smile. She longed to reach out and touch him. But she dared not, for she knew that, if she were to touch him now, she would need to hang on to him forever. It would demand a great deal more strength than she possessed to release him.

She went on, her voice sounding remarkably normal, 'We both made the mistake of believing my sister... when she was in what might charitably be called a less than sterling frame of mind.'

Roth smiled at that. 'But she seems to have improved...' With his free hand he touched his inside pocket. 'I have a letter from her here. It was posted a couple of weeks ago, though it didn't actually reach me until a few days ago...'

He smiled. 'I've been incommunicado, too busy trying to find you...' Then he continued, 'The letter is an apology for everything that happened, and a plea not to believe that you were in any way involved in, or even remotely knew about, what she was up to. But, as I told you, I'd already come to that conclusion myself.'

'Rita did that?' Luisa felt gratified at the gesture. But not as gratified as she felt at Roth's confession.

She narrowed her eyes at him. 'Have you really been incommunicado? Have you really been searching for me as seriously as that?'

'It's been my number one preoccupation for the past three weeks.' He stood back a little, his expression serious, and let his dark gaze pour down on her. 'Tell me, Luisa... Are you glad I found you?'

It was in that moment, as she gazed back at him, that Luisa's fear fell away from her. What she had seen in his eyes she had not imagined. For there was no denying the tenderness that shone from them now.

With a sense of joy she reached out her hand and touched him. 'I've never been more glad about anything in my life.'

He smiled then. 'You mean that?'

Luisa nodded. 'I mean it.' Then she tilted her head at him. 'And are you glad that you've found me?'

He did not answer for a moment, but simply gazed down at her in wonder. Then he was gathering her to him, his arms folding round her, holding her as though he would never let her go.

'Oh, I'm glad! You can believe it!' He kissed her hair softly, then tilted her chin to look down into her eyes. 'And now I can tell you the other reason

I had to find you. To ask your forgiveness was only the first part...'

Luisa's hand was against his cheek. As he turned quickly to kiss it, she felt her heart turn over and brush against her ribs. And as he opened his mouth to speak, she held her breath and waited.

'The other reason was to tell you that I love you...'

He kissed her hand again.

'...and to ask you to marry me.'

Luisa gazed at him in silence, overcome with emotion, as a well of purest happiness suddenly rose up inside her.

Then she reached up and kissed him. 'I'll marry you,' she told him. 'And I'll love you for all the days of my life.'

'Oh, Luisa...! My Luisa! You don't know how happy you've made me!'

With a whoop of joy, he lifted her clean off the floor. Then his lips were crushing hers and her arms were round his neck, and suddenly the very air all about them was filled with the love and the joy that flowed between them.

Roth paused to snatch a breath. 'How does next week sound for the wedding?'

'This is sinful, you know!'

Luisa sat up with a smile amid the tangle of silk sheets on the huge gold bed. 'Twice is really inexcusable. It's too much for anyone!'

'This is the first complaint I've heard.' Roth, lying beside her, reached out and stroked her naked back with his finger. 'Don't tell me you're going off sex already?'

'I didn't mean that!' Luisa turned round and caught his hand and gave his fingers a playful tweak. 'You know very well I wasn't meaning that!'

'I'm glad to hear it!' He laughed and drew her down against him, his arms folding round her, wrapping her in his nakedness. 'After all, there's nothing sinful about it, however often we do it. You and I, my dear young lady, are married.'

What an astounding notion! Luisa was still getting used to it. Two weeks had passed since their wedding in London, the most exciting, most joyful two weeks of her life. But it still felt like a dream each time she looked into Roth's eyes and realised with a start of happiness that he was hers now forever. It was almost too much happiness for her heart to cope with.

She looked into his eyes now, seeing the love that shone there, and cast her mind back to that wonderful day when the two of them had become man and wife.

It had been a quiet affair, kept secret from the media—her decision as much as Roth's!—but it had been a wonderful day that she would treasure forever. All her friends had been there, and most of her family—though, alas, not Rita and Alan and the children.

'It would be better if we didn't come,' Rita had insisted when Luisa had phoned her with the invitation. 'I appreciate you asking me and I wish you all the best. Maybe, later, when time has passed, we can all try to be friends.'

Luisa hoped so. Certainly, from Roth's side there were no hard feelings, though she could appreciate that for Rita and Alan things were more tricky. It was from their side, after all, that had come all the lies and deception.

For there were more lies, Luisa had discovered, than the lies surrounding the supposed affair.

Alan had lied, too. He had lied to Luisa about why Roth had sacked him from the company. For it had not been out of spite, as he had suggested. It had been because Roth had discovered he was stealing.

Roth had smiled wryly when he'd told her, 'At least it means he'll be able to foot the bill for his wife's little brainstorm in the Bahamas!'

Indeed! Luisa had wondered where that money would come from. According to Rita, her credit card was almost worn out!

So, Luisa had accepted her sister's decision without arguing. It would take time to mend all the bridges that had been broken. But, in time, she felt certain, they *would* be mended.

She smiled down now at Roth. He was the reason she felt so certain. With Roth, she was discovering, all good things were possible.

With a sigh she kissed his face. 'How happy you make me. I never believed it was possible to be happy like this.'

'That's what I'm here for.' He returned her kiss, softly. 'I'm here to make my wonderful, beautiful wife happy. After all, it's no more than she does for me.'

He smoothed back her hair and smiled into her face. 'So, what were you saying about sin just a moment ago?'

Luisa laughed. 'I was saying it was almost sinful... Two holidays in the Bahamas in the space of a few months. At this rate, you're going to spoil me rotten!'

'I fully intend to.' He smiled and tugged her against him. 'To make you happy and spoil you rotten, these are my two main ambitions.' He kissed her nose. 'Do you have any complaints?'

'None.' Luisa giggled as she slipped her arms round his neck, running her fingers through the thick, silky hair. 'Besides, I know better than to try and stop you,' she told him. 'I know what you're like when your mind's made up.'

'Unstoppable!' Roth laughed and rolled her over, so that now she was under him and he was leaning over her. And suddenly there was a dark, smoky look in his eyes that caused a finger of excitement to flicker against her.

'By the way,' he growled, 'there's something else I have on my mind.' He smiled. 'Unless, of course, you think that would be sinful?'

'I think it might be.' She pretended to pull a face. Then, as he pressed against her, sending flames shooting through her, she tangled her fingers tightly in his hair. 'But it just so happens that there's nothing in the world I enjoy more than being sinful with you.'

'Good. Because I'm planning on our leading a disgracefully sinful life.'

Luisa smiled. 'I'm pleased to hear it. That rather coincides with my own plans.'

'Really?'

'Absolutely. A disgracefully sinful life.'

Roth gazed into her eyes, the love and longing in him pouring down on her like warm sunshine. 'I think,' he said, 'that bodes well for the future. I think you and I are at the start of something pretty sensational.'

'I think we are.' Luisa hugged him and held him close to her, her heart overflowing with love and happiness. 'The most sensational love-affair in the history of the universe.'

And, as Roth smiled down at her, she knew she was right.

Accept 4 FREE Romances and 2 FREE gifts

FROM READER SERVICE

Here's an irresistible invitation from Mills & Boon. Please accept our offer of 4 FREE Romances, a CUDDLY TEDDY and a special MYSTERY GIFT! Then, if you choose, go on to enjoy 6 captivating Romances every month for just £1.80 each, postage and packing FREE. Plus our FREE Newsletter with author news, competitions and much more.

**Send the coupon below to:
Mills & Boon Reader Service,
FREEPOST, PO Box 236,
Croydon, Surrey CR9 9EL.**

NO STAMP REQUIRED

Yes! Please rush me 4 FREE Romances and 2 FREE gifts! Please also reserve me a Reader Service subscription. If I decide to subscribe I can look forward to receiving 6 brand new Romances for just £10.80 each month, post and packing FREE. If I decide not to subscribe I shall write to you within 10 days - I can keep the free books and gifts whatever I choose. I may cancel or suspend my subscription at any time. I am over 18 years of age.

Ms/Mrs/Miss/Mr _____ EP55R

Address _____

_____

Postcode _____ Signature _____

Offer closes 31st March 1994. The right is reserved to refuse an application and change the terms of this offer. One application per household. Overseas readers please write for details. Southern Africa write to Book Services International Ltd., Box 41654, Craighall, Transvaal 2024.
You may be mailed with offers from other reputable companies as a result of this application. Please tick box if you would prefer not to receive such offers ☐

mps MAILING PREFERENCE SERVICE

FOR BETTER
FOR WORSE

An unforgettable story of broken dreams and new beginnings

Penny Jordan is set to take the bestseller lists by storm again this autumn, with her stunning new novel which is a masterpiece of raw emotion.

A story of obsessions...
A story of choices...
A story of love.

LARGE-FORMAT
PAPERBACK AVAILABLE
FROM NOVEMBER

PRICED: £8.99

WORLDWIDE

Available from W.H. Smith, John Menzies, Martins, Forbuoys, most supermarkets and other paperback stockists. Also available from Worldwide Reader Service, Freepost, PO Box 236, Thornton Road, Croydon, Surrey CR9 9EL. (UK Postage & Packing free)

Next Month's Romances

Each month you can choose from a wide variety of romance with Mills & Boon. Below are the new titles to look out for next month, why not ask either Mills & Boon Reader Service or your Newsagent to reserve you a copy of the titles you want to buy – just tick the titles you would like and either post to Reader Service or take it to any Newsagent and ask them to order your books.

Please save me the following titles:		Please tick √
UNWILLING MISTRESS	Lindsay Armstrong	
DARK HERITAGE	Emma Darcy	
WOUNDS OF PASSION	Charlotte Lamb	
LOST IN LOVE	Michelle Reid	
ORIGINAL SIN	Rosalie Ash	
SUDDEN FIRE	Elizabeth Oldfield	
THE BRIDE OF SANTA BARBARA	Angela Devine	
ISLAND OF SHELLS	Grace Green	
LOVE'S REVENGE	Mary Lyons	
MAKING MAGIC	Karen van der Zee	
OASIS OF THE HEART	Jessica Hart	
BUILD A DREAM	Quinn Wilder	
A BRIDE TO LOVE	Barbara McMahon	
A MAN CALLED TRAVERS	Brittany Young	
A CHILD CALLED MATTHEW	Sara Grant	
DANCE OF SEDUCTION	Vanessa Grant	

If you would like to order these books in addition to your regular subscription from Mills & Boon Reader Service please send £1.80 per title to: Mills & Boon Reader Service, Freepost, P.O. Box 236, Croydon, Surrey, CR9 9EL, quote your Subscriber No:.................................. (If applicable) and complete the name and address details below. Alternatively, these books are available from many local Newsagents including W.H.Smith, J.Menzies, Martins and other paperback stockists from 14 January 1994.

Name:..
Address:..
....Post Code:........................

To Retailer: If you would like to stock M&B books please contact your regular book/magazine wholesaler for details.

You may be mailed with offers from other reputable companies as a result of this application.
If you would rather not take advantage of these opportunities please tick box ☐